ONCE TAKEN

(A RILEY PAIGE MYSTERY—BOOK 2)

BLAKE PIERCE

ISBN: 978-1-63291-564-1

BOOKS BY BLAKE PIERCE

RILEY PAIGE MYSTERY SERIES

Prologue

Captain Jimmy Cole had just finished telling his passengers an old Hudson River ghost story. It was a good one, about an ax murderer in a long, dark coat, perfect for a foggy night like this. He sat back in his chair and rested his knees for a moment, too creaky from too many surgeries, and pondered, for the millionth time, his retirement. He'd seen nearly every hamlet the Hudson had to offer, and one of these days, even a small fishing boat like his, the *Suzy*, would get the best of him.

Done for the night, he steered his ship for shore, and as it chugged steadily for the dock at Reedsport, one of his passengers called out, jarring him from his reverie.

"Hey, Cap'n—isn't that your ghost right over there?"

Jimmy didn't bother to look. All four of his passengers—two young vacationing couples—were pretty drunk. Doubtless one of the guys was just trying to scare the girls.

But then one of the women added: "I see it too. Isn't it weird?"

Jimmy turned toward his passengers. Goddamn drunks. Last time he'd charter his boat this late at night.

The second man pointed.

"It's over there," he said.

His wife covered her eyes.

"Oh, I can't look!" she said with a nervous and embarrassed laugh.

Jimmy, exasperated, realizing he wasn't going to get any rest, finally turned and looked where the man was pointing.

In a gap between the shoreline trees, something did catch his eye. It glistened, he thought, and it had a vaguely human shape. Whatever it was, it seemed to float above the ground. But it was too far away to see clearly.

Before Jimmy could reach for his binoculars, the object disappeared behind the trees along the bank.

The truth was, Jimmy had had a few beers himself. That wasn't a problem as far as he was concerned. He knew this river well. And he liked his job. He especially enjoyed being out on the Hudson at this time of night, when the water was so still and peaceful. Few things out here could shatter his sense of calm.

He slowed and steered the *Suzy* carefully against the bumpers as he hit the dock. Proud of himself for a gentle landing, he stopped the engine and lashed the boat to the cleats.

The passengers tumbled off the boat giggling and laughing.

They staggered down the dock to shore and headed toward their B&B. Jimmy was glad they'd paid in advance.

But he couldn't stop thinking about that strange object he'd spotted. It was far back down the shoreline and impossible to see from here. Who or what might it be?

Annoyed by it, he knew he wouldn't get any rest until he figured it out. That was just the way he was.

Jimmy sighed loudly, twice as annoyed, and set off on foot, trudging back along the riverbank, following the train tracks that bordered the water. Those tracks had been in use a hundred years ago when Reedsport was mostly bordellos and gambling houses. Now, they were just another relic to a bygone time.

Jimmy finally rounded a curve and approached an old warehouse near the tracks. A few security lamps on the building cast a dim light, and he saw it: a glistening human shape that seemed to be floating in mid-air. The shape was suspended from one of the crossbeams of a power pole.

As he neared and got a good look, a chill ran up his spine. The shape was truly human—yet it didn't show any signs of life. The body faced away from him, bound in some kind of fabric and wrapped around and around with heavy chains that crisscrossed and connected far beyond any need to hold a prisoner. The chains glittered in the light.

Oh, God, not again.

Jimmy could not help but remember a gruesome murder that had rocked the whole area several years ago.

His knees weakening, Jimmy walked around to the other side of the body. He stepped close enough to see its face—and he almost fell to the tracks in shock. He recognized her. It was a local woman, a nurse, and a friend of many years. Her throat was slashed, and her dead mouth was gagged open with a chain that wrapped around her head.

Jimmy gasped in grief and horror.

The murderer was back.

2

Chapter 1

Special Agent Riley Paige froze in place, staring in shock. The handful of pebbles on her bed shouldn't have been there. Someone had broken into her home and placed them—someone who meant her harm.

She knew immediately the pebbles were a message, and that the message was from an old enemy. He was telling her that she had not killed him after all.

Peterson is alive.

She felt her body tremble at the thought.

She'd long suspected it, and now she was absolutely sure. Worse, he'd been inside her house. The thought made her want to throw up. Was he still here now?

Her breathing became short with fear. Riley knew that her physical resources were limited. Just that day she had survived a deadly encounter with a sadistic killer, and her head was still bandaged and her body bruised all over. Would she be ready to face him if he were inside her house?

Riley immediately drew her gun from its holster. Hands trembling, she went to her closet and opened it. Nobody was in there. She checked under her bed. Nobody there either.

Riley stood there and forced herself to think clearly. Had she been in the bedroom since she had gotten home? Yes, she had, because she had put her gun holster on top of the dresser next to the door. But she hadn't turned on the light and hadn't even looked into the room. She had simply stepped into the doorway and deposited her weapon on the dresser top, then left. She'd changed into her nightgown in the bathroom.

Could her nemesis have been in the house this whole time? After she and April got home, the two of them had talked and watched TV late into the night. Then April had gone to bed. In a tiny house like hers, staying hidden would require amazing stealth. But she couldn't discount the possibility.

Then she was seized by a new fear.

April!

Riley snatched the flashlight that she kept on the side table. With her gun in her right hand and the flashlight in her left, she stepped out of her bedroom and switched on the hall light. When she heard nothing awry, she quickly made her way to April's bedroom and threw open the door. The room was pitch dark. Riley turned on the overhead light.

Her daughter was already in bed.

3

"What is it, Mom?" April asked, squinting with surprise.

Riley stepped into the bedroom.

"Don't get out of bed," she said. "Stay right where you are."

"Mom, you're scaring me," April said, her voice trembling.

That was just fine as far as Riley was concerned. She was plenty scared herself, and her daughter had every reason to be as scared as she was. She went to April's closet, shined her flashlight around inside, and saw that no one was there. No one was under April's bed either.

What should she do next? She had to check every nook and corner in the rest of the house.

Riley knew what her one-time partner Bill Jeffreys would say.

Damn it, Riley, call for help.

Her longstanding tendency to go things alone had always infuriated Bill. But this time, she was going to heed his advice. With April in the house, Riley wasn't going to take any chances.

"Put on a bathrobe and some shoes," she said to her daughter. "But don't leave this room—not yet."

Riley went back into her bedroom and picked up her phone from the side table. She punched autodial for the Behavioral Analysis Unit. As soon as she heard a voice on the line, she hissed, "This is Special Agent Riley Paige. There's been an intruder in my home. He might still be here. I need someone here fast." She thought for a second, then added, "And send an evidence team."

"We'll get right on it," came the reply.

Riley ended the phone call and stepped out into the hall again. Except for the two bedrooms and the hallway, the house was still dark. He could be anywhere, lurking, waiting to attack. This man had caught her off guard once before, and she had nearly died at his hands.

Switching lights on as she went and keeping her gun at the ready, Riley moved efficiently through the house. She aimed her flashlight into every closet and unlit corner.

Finally, she glanced up at the hallway ceiling. The door above her led to the attic, with a pull-down ladder tucked away inside. Did she dare climb up there for a look?

At that moment Riley heard police sirens. She breathed a huge sigh of relief at the sound. She realized that the agency had called in the local police, because BAU headquarters was more than half an hour away.

She went to her bedroom and pulled on a pair of shoes and her bathrobe, then returned to April's room.

4

"Come with me," she said. "Stay close."

Still holding her gun, Riley wrapped her left arm around April's shoulders. The poor girl was trembling with fear. Riley led April to the front door and opened it just as several uniformed police officers came dashing up the sidewalk.

The male officer in charge came into the house, his gun drawn.

"What's the problem?" he asked.

"Someone was in the house," Riley said. "He might still be here."

The officer eyed the gun in her hand uneasily.

"I'm FBI," Riley said. "BAU agents will be here soon. I've already searched the house, except the attic." She pointed. "There's a door in the ceiling over in the hall."

The officer called out, "Bowers, Wright, get in here and check the attic. The rest of you search outside, back and front."

Bowers and Wright went straight to the hallway and pulled down the ladder. Both drew their weapons. One waited at the bottom of the ladder while the other climbed upward and flashed a light around. In a few moments, the man disappeared into the attic.

Soon a voice called out, "No one here."

Riley wanted to feel relieved. But the truth was, she more than half wished that Peterson had been up there. He could be arrested right here and now—or better yet, shot. She was all but sure that he wasn't going to turn up in the front yard or the back.

"Have you got a basement?" the lead officer asked.

"No, just a crawl space," Riley said.

The officer called outside, "Benson, Pratt, check under the house."

April was still holding onto her mother for dear life.

"What's going on, Mom?" she asked.

Riley hesitated. For years she'd avoided telling April much of the ugly truth about her work. But she had recently realized that she'd been overly protective. So she'd told April about her traumatic captivity at Peterson's hands—or at least as much as she thought she could handle. She'd also confided her doubts that the man was really dead.

But what should she tell April now? She wasn't sure.

Before Riley could make up her mind, April said, "It's Peterson, isn't it?"

Riley hugged her daughter tightly. She nodded back, trying to hide the shiver that ran through her whole body.

"He's still alive."

5

Chapter 2

An hour later, Riley's house was swarming with people wearing uniforms or FBI labels. Heavily armed Federal agents and an evidence team were working with the police.

"Bag those pebbles on the bed," Craig Huang called out. "They'll need to be examined for prints or DNA."

At first, Riley hadn't been pleased to see that Huang was in charge. He was very young, and her previous experience working with him hadn't gone well. But now she saw that he was giving solid orders and organizing the scene effectively. Huang was growing into his job.

The evidence team was already at work combing every inch of the house and dusting for fingerprints. Other agents had disappeared into the darkness behind the house, trying to find vehicle tracks or some hint of a trail through the woods. Now that things seemed to be running smoothly, Huang led Riley away from the others into the kitchen. He and Riley sat down at the table. April joined them there, still badly shaken.

"So what do you think?" Huang asked Riley. "Is there any chance that we'll still find him?"

Riley sighed with discouragement.

"No, I'm afraid he's long gone. He must have been here earlier this evening, before my daughter and I got home."

Just then a Kevlar-clad female agent came in from the back of the house. She had dark hair, dark eyes, and a dark complexion, and she looked even younger than Huang.

"Agent Huang, I found something," the woman said. "Scratches on the back door lock. It looks like someone picked it open."

"Good work, Vargas," Huang said. "Now we know how he got in. Could you stay with Riley and her daughter for a little while?"

The young woman's face lit up with delight.

"I'll be glad to," she said.

She sat at the table, and Huang left the kitchen to rejoin the others.

"Agent Paige, I'm Agent María de la Luz Vargas Ramírez." Then she grinned. "I know, it's a mouthful. It's a Mexican thing. People call me Lucy Vargas."

"I'm glad you're here, Agent Vargas," Riley said.

"Just Lucy, please."

The young woman fell silent for a moment and just kept gazing

6

at Riley. Finally she said, "Agent Paige, I hope I'm not out of line in saying this, but … it's a real honor to meet you. I've been following your work ever since I went into training. Your whole record is just so amazing."

"Thank you," Riley said.

Lucy smiled with admiration. "I mean, the way you wrapped up the Peterson case—the whole story just amazes me."

Riley shook her head.

"I wish things were that simple," she said. "He's not dead. He was the intruder here today."

Lucy stared back, stunned.

"But everybody says—" Lucy began.

Riley interrupted.

"Someone else thought he was alive. Marie, the woman I rescued. She was sure he was still out there taunting her. She …"

Riley paused, painfully remembering the sight of Marie's body hanging in her own bedroom.

"She committed suicide," Riley said.

Lucy looked both horrified and surprised. "I'm sorry," she said.

Just then, Riley heard a familiar voice call out to her.

"Riley? You okay?"

She turned and saw Bill Jeffreys standing in the kitchen archway, looking anxious. The BAU must have alerted him about the trouble, so he'd driven here on his own.

"I'm okay, Bill," she said. "So is April. Sit down."

Bill sat down at the table with Riley, April, and Lucy. Lucy stared at him, apparently in awe to meet Riley's former partner, yet another FBI legend.

Huang stepped back into the kitchen.

"Nobody's in the house, or outside either," he told Riley. "My people have gathered up whatever evidence they can find. They say it won't be much to go on. It'll be up to the lab technicians to see what they can make of it."

"I was afraid of that," Riley said.

"Looks like it's time for us to wrap things up for tonight," Huang said. Then he left the kitchen to give his final orders to the agents.

Riley turned toward her daughter.

"April, you're going to stay at your father's house tonight."

April's eyes widened.

"I'm not leaving you here," April said. "And I sure don't want to stay with Dad."

"You've got to," Riley said. "You might not be safe here."

"But Mom—"

Riley interrupted. "April, there are still things I haven't told you about this man. Terrible things. You'll be safe with your father. I'll pick you up tomorrow after your class."

Before April could protest further, Lucy spoke.

"Your mother's right, April. Take it from me. In fact, consider it an order from me. I'll handpick a couple of agents who can drive you there. Agent Paige, with your permission, I'll call your ex-husband and tell him what's going on."

Riley was surprised by Lucy's offer. She was also pleased. Almost uncannily, Lucy seemed to understand that this would be an awkward call for her to make. Ryan would undoubtedly take this news more seriously from any agent other than Riley. Lucy had also handled April well.

Not only had Lucy had spotted the picked lock, she also demonstrated empathy. Empathy was an excellent quality in a BAU agent, and it was all too often worn away by the stress of the job.

This woman is good, Riley thought.

"Come on," Lucy said to April. "Let's go call your dad."

April stared daggers at Riley. Even so, she got up from the table and followed Lucy into the living room, where they started making the call.

Riley and Bill were left sitting at the kitchen table alone. Even though there seemed to be nothing left to do, it seemed right to Riley that Bill was there. They had worked together for years and she had always thought of them as something like a matched pair— both were forty with touches of gray showing in dark hair. They were both dedicated to their jobs and troubled in their marriages. Bill was solid in build and temperament.

"It was Peterson," Riley said. "He was here."

Bill said nothing. He looked unconvinced.

"You don't believe me?" Riley said. "There were pebbles in my bed. He must have put them there. They couldn't have gotten there any other way."

Bill shook his head.

"Riley, I'm sure there really was an intruder," he said. "You weren't imagining that part. But Peterson? I doubt that very much."

Riley's anger was rising now.

"Bill, listen to me. I heard rattling against the door one night, and I looked outside, and I found pebbles there. Marie heard someone throw pebbles at her bedroom window. Who else could it be?"

Bill sighed and shook his head.

"Riley, you're tired," he said. "And when you're tired and you get an idea fixed in your head, it's easy to believe just about anything. It can happen to anybody."

Riley found herself fighting back tears. In better days, Bill would have trusted her instincts without question. But those days were over. And she knew why. A few nights ago she'd called him drunk and suggested that they act on their mutual attraction and begin an affair. It had been an awful thing to do, and she knew it, and she'd not had a drink since then. Even so, things hadn't been right between her and Bill after that.

"I know what this is about, Bill," she said. "It's because of that stupid phone call. You don't trust me anymore."

Now Bill's voice crackled with anger.

"Damn it, Riley, I'm just trying to be realistic."

Riley was seething. "Just go, Bill."

"But Riley—"

"Believe me or don't believe me. Take your pick. But right now I want you to go."

With an air of resignation, Bill got up from the table and left.

Through the kitchen doorway, Riley could see that almost everybody had left the house, including April. Lucy came back into the kitchen.

"Agent Huang is leaving a couple of agents here," she said. "They'll watch the house from a car for the rest of the night. I'm not sure it's a good idea for you to be alone inside. I'll be glad to stay."

Riley sat and thought for a moment. What she wanted—what she *needed* right now—was for somebody to believe that Peterson wasn't dead. She doubted that she could convince even Lucy of that. The whole thing seemed hopeless.

"I'll be all right, Lucy," Riley said.

Lucy nodded and left the kitchen. Riley heard the sound of the last agents leaving the house and shutting the door behind them. Riley got up and checked both the front door and back door to make sure they were locked. She moved two chairs up against the back door. They would make noise enough if anybody picked the lock again.

Then she stood in the living room and looked all around. The house looked weirdly bright, with every single light burning.

I ought to turn some of them off, she thought.

But as she reached for the living room light switch, her fingers froze. She just couldn't do it. She was paralyzed with terror. Peterson, she knew, was coming for her again.

Chapter 3

Riley hesitated for a moment as she entered the BAU building, wondering if she was really ready to face anyone today. She hadn't slept all night, and was bone-tired. The sensation of terror that had kept her awake all night had run her adrenaline until there was nothing left. Now, she just felt hollowed out.

Riley took a deep breath.

The only way out is through.

She gathered her resolve and walked into the busy maze of FBI agents, specialists, and support staff. As she wound her way through the open bay area, familiar faces looked up from their computers. Most smiled to see her and several gave her a thumbs-up. Riley slowly felt glad she had decided to come in. She'd needed something to lift to her spirits.

"Way to go with the Dolly Killer," one young agent said.

It took Riley a couple of seconds to understand what he meant. Then she realized that "Dolly Killer" must be the new nickname for Dirk Monroe, the psychopath she had just taken down. The name made sense.

Riley also noticed that some of the faces looked at her more warily. Doubtless they had heard about the incident at her house last night when a whole team had raced to her frantic call for backup. *They probably wonder if I'm in my right mind,* she thought. As far as she knew, absolutely no one else in the Bureau believed that Peterson was still alive.

Riley stopped by the desk of Sam Flores, a lab technician with black-rimmed glasses, hard at work at his computer.

"What news have you got for me, Sam?" Riley said.

Sam looked up from the screen at her.

"You mean about your break-in, right? I'm just now looking at some preliminary reports. I'm afraid there won't be much. The lab guys didn't get anything off the pebbles—no DNA or fibers. No fingerprints, either."

Riley sighed with discouragement.

"Let me know if anything changes," she said, patting Flores on the back.

"I wouldn't count on it," Flores said.

Riley continued on to the area shared by senior agents. As she passed by the small glass-walled offices, she saw that Bill wasn't in. That was actually a relief, but she knew that sooner or later she would have to clear up the recent awkwardness between them.

11

When she set foot in her own neat, well-organized office, Riley immediately noticed that she had a phone message. It was from Mike Nevins, the D.C. forensic psychiatrist who sometimes consulted on BAU cases. Over the years, she had found him a source remarkable insight, and not only into cases. Mike had helped Riley through her own bout of PTSD after Peterson had captured and tortured her. She knew he was calling to check up on her, as he often did.

She was about to call him back, when the broad frame of Special Agent Brent Meredith appeared in her doorway. The unit commander's black, angular features hinted at his tough, no-nonsense personality. Riley felt relieved at the sight of him, always reassured by his presence.

"Welcome back, Agent Paige," he said.

Riley got up to shake his hand. "Thanks, Agent Meredith."

"I hear you had another little adventure last night. I hope you're all right."

"I'm fine, thanks."

Meredith looked at her with warm concern, and Riley knew that he was trying to assess her readiness for work.

"Would you like to join me in the break area for some coffee?" he asked.

"Thanks, but there are some files I really need to review. Some other time."

Meredith nodded and said nothing. Riley knew he was waiting for her to speak. Doubtless he had also heard about her belief that Peterson had been the intruder. He was giving her a chance to voice her opinion. But she was sure that Meredith wouldn't be any more inclined than anybody else to agree with her about Peterson.

"Well, I'd better be going," he said. "Let me know whenever you're up for coffee or lunch."

"I'll do that."

Meredith paused and turned back toward Riley.

Slowly and carefully, he said, "Do be careful, Agent Paige."

Riley detected a world of meaning in those words. Not long ago, another higher-up in the agency had suspended her for subordination. She'd been reinstated, but her position could be still tenuous. Riley sensed that Meredith was giving her a friendly warning. He didn't want her to do anything to jeopardize herself. And raising a lot of fuss about Peterson might cause trouble with those who had declared the case closed.

As soon as she was alone, Riley went to her filing cabinet and pulled out the thick file on the Peterson case. She opened it up on her desk and browsed through it, refreshing her memory about her nemesis. She didn't find much that was helpful.

The truth was that the man remained an enigma. There hadn't even been any records of his existence until Bill and Riley finally tracked him down. Peterson might not even be his real name, and they'd turned up several different first names supposedly connected with him.

As Riley looked through the file, she came across photographs of his victims—women who had been found in shallow graves. They had all borne burn scars, and the cause of death had been manual strangulation. Riley shuddered with the memory of the large, powerful hands that had caught her and caged her like an animal.

Nobody knew just how many women he had killed. There might be many more corpses yet to be found. And until Marie and Riley had been captured and lived to tell about it, nobody knew about how he liked to torment women in the dark with a propane torch. And nobody else was willing to believe that Peterson was still alive.

The whole thing was really getting her down. Riley was known for her ability to get into the minds of killers—an ability that sometimes scared her. Even so, she'd never been able to get into Peterson's mind. And as of right now, she felt that she understood him even less.

He had never struck Riley as an organized psychopath. The fact that he left his victims in shallow graves suggested quite the opposite. He was no perfectionist. Even so, he was meticulous enough not to leave clues behind. The man was truly paradoxical.

She remembered something that Marie had said to her shortly before her suicide …

"Maybe he's like a ghost, Riley. Maybe that's what happened when you blew him up. You killed his body but you didn't kill his evil."

He wasn't a ghost, and Riley knew it. She was sure—more sure than ever—that he was out there, and that she was his next target. Even so, he might as well be a ghost as far as she was concerned. Aside from herself, nobody else even believed that he existed.

"Where are you, you bastard?" she whispered aloud.

She didn't know, and she had no way to find out. She was completely stymied. She had no choice but to let the whole thing go for now. She closed the folder and put it back in its place in her

13

filing cabinet.

Then her office phone rang. She saw that the call was coming through on a line shared by all the special agents. It was the line that the BAU phone bank used to forward appropriate call-ins to agents. As a rule of thumb, whichever agent picked up such a call first would take the case.

Riley glanced around at the other offices. Nobody else seemed to be in at the moment. The other agents were all either taking a break or out working other cases. Riley answered the phone.

"Special Agent Riley Paige. What can I do to help you?"

The voice on the line sounded harried.

"Agent Paige, this is Raymond Alford, Chief of Police in Reedsport, New York. We've got a real problem here. Would it be okay for us to do this by video chat? I think maybe I could explain it better. And I've got some images that you'd better see for yourself."

Riley's curiosity was piqued. "Certainly," she said. She gave Alford her contact information. A few moments later she was talking to him face to face. He was a slender, balding man who appeared to be well along in years. At the moment, his expression was anxious and tired.

"We had a murder here last night," Alford told her. "A real ugly one. Let me show you."

A photograph came up on Riley's computer screen. It showed what appeared to be a woman's body hanging from a chain over railroad tracks. The body was wrapped in a multitude of chains, and it seemed to be oddly dressed.

"What's the victim wearing?" Riley asked.

"A straitjacket," Alford said.

Riley was startled. Looking closer at the photograph, she could see that it was true. Then the picture disappeared, and Riley found herself face to face with Alford again.

"Chief Alford, I appreciate your alarm. But what makes you think this is a case for the Behavioral Analysis Unit?"

"Because this exact same thing happened very near here five years ago," Alford said.

An image appeared of another woman's corpse. She, too, was chained all over and bound in a straitjacket.

"Back then it was a part-time prison worker, Marla Blainey. The MO was identical—except that she was just dumped on the riverbank, not hung up."

Alford's face reappeared.

14

"This time it was Rosemary Pickens, a local nurse," he said. "Nobody can imagine a motive, not for either of the women. They were both well-liked."

Alford slumped wearily and shook his head.

"Agent Paige, my people and I are really out of our depth here. This new killing must be a serial or copycat. The trouble is, neither of those makes any sense. We don't get that kind of problem in Reedsport. This is just a little Hudson River tourist town with a population of about seven thousand. Sometimes we have to break up a fight or fish a tourist out of the river. That's about as bad as things usually get here."

Riley thought about it. This actually did look like a case for the BAU. She really ought to refer Alford directly to Meredith.

But Riley glanced toward Meredith's office and saw that he hadn't returned yet. She'd have to alert him about this later. In the meantime, maybe she could help a little.

"What were the causes of death?" she asked.

"Throats slashed, both of them."

Riley tried not to show her surprise. Strangulation and blunt force strike were far more common than slashing.

This seemed to be a highly unusual killer. Even so, it was the kind of psychopath that Riley knew well. She specialized in just such cases. It seemed a shame that she wasn't going to be able to bring her skills to this one. In the wake of her recent trauma, she wouldn't get the assignment.

"Have you taken the body down?" Riley asked.

"Not yet," Alford said. "She's still hanging there."

"Then don't. Leave it there for now. Wait till our agents get there."

Alford didn't look pleased.

"Agent Paige, that's going to be a tall order. It's right next to the train tracks and it can be seen from the river. And the town doesn't need this kind of publicity. I'm under a lot of pressure to take it down."

"Leave it," Riley said. "I know it's not easy, but it's important. It won't be long. We'll get agents there this afternoon."

Alford nodded in mute compliance.

"Have you got any more photos of the latest victim?" Riley asked. "Any close-ups?"

"Sure, I'll bring them up."

Riley found herself looking at a series of detail shots of the corpse. The local cops had done a good job. The photos showed

15

how tightly and elaborately the chains were wrapped around the corpse.

Finally came a close-up of the victim's face.

Riley felt as though her heart jumped up into her throat. The victim's eyes bulged, and her mouth was gagged by a chain. But that wasn't what shocked Riley.

The woman looked a lot like Marie. She was older and heavier, but even so, Marie might have looked a lot like this if she'd only lived another decade or so. The image hit Riley like an emotional blow to the gut. It was as if Marie was calling out for her, demanding that she get this killer.

She knew that she had to take this case.

Chapter 4

Peterson coasted his car along, not too fast, not too slow, feeling good as he finally had the girl back in his sights. Finally, he had found her. There she was, Riley's daughter, alone, walking toward her high school, with no clue at all that he was stalking her. That he was about to end her life.

As he watched, she suddenly stopped in her tracks and turned around, as if suspicious she were being watched. She stood there, as if undecided. A few other students passed her and filtered into the building.

He coasted the car along, waiting to see what she would do next.

Not that the girl mattered to him especially. Her mother was the true target of his revenge. Her mother had thwarted him badly, and she had to pay. She already had, in a way—after all, he'd driven Marie Sayles to suicide. But now he had to take from her the girl who mattered to her most.

The girl, to his delight, began to turn around and walk away from school. Apparently she had decided not to go to class today. His heart pounded—he wanted to pounce. But he could not. Not yet. He had to tell himself to be patient. Other people were still in sight.

Peterson drove ahead and circled a block, forcing himself to be patient. He suppressed a smile at the joy to come. With what he had in mind for her daughter, Riley would suffer in ways she didn't think possible. Although she was still gangly and awkward, the girl looked a lot like her mother. That would make it extra satisfying.

As he circled around, he saw that the girl was walking briskly along the street. He pulled over to the curb and watched her for a few minutes, until he realized that she was taking a road that led out of town. If she was going to walk home alone, then this might be the perfect moment to take control of her.

His heart pounding, wanting to savor the delightful anticipation, Peterson circled another block with his car.

People needed to learn to put off certain pleasures, Peterson knew, to wait until just the right time. Delayed gratification made everything more pleasurable. He had learned that from years of delicious, lingering cruelty.

There's just so much to look forward to, he thought contentedly.

When he came back around and saw her again, Peterson

17

laughed aloud. She was hitchhiking! God was smiling down upon him on this day. Taking her life was clearly meant to be.

He pulled the car up beside her and gave her his most pleasant smile.

"Give you a lift?"

The girl smiled back broadly. "Thanks. That would be great."

"Where are you headed?" he asked.

"I live just a little way out of town."

The girl told him the address.

He said, "I'm going right past there. Hop in."

The girl got into the front seat. With increasing satisfaction, he observed that she even had her mother's hazel eyes.

Peterson pressed the buttons to lock the doors and windows. Over the quiet rumble of the air conditioner, the girl didn't even notice.

*

April felt a pleasant rush of adrenaline as she fastened the safety harness. She'd never hitchhiked before. Her mother would have a fit if she found out.

Of course, it served Mom right, April figured. It was really rotten to make her stay at Dad's last night—and all because of some crazy idea of hers that Peterson had been in their home. It wasn't true, and April knew it. The two agents who had driven her to Dad's house had said so. From what they'd said to each other, it sounded kind of like the whole agency thought Mom was a bit bonkers.

The man said, "So what brings you into Fredericksburg?"

April turned and looked at him. He was an agreeable-looking, big-jawed guy with shaggy hair and a stubble of beard. He was smiling.

"School," April said.

"A summer class?" the man asked.

"Yeah," April said. She certainly wasn't going to tell him that she'd decided to skip the class. Not that he looked like the kind of guy who wouldn't understand. He seemed pretty cool. Maybe he'd even get a kick out of helping her defy parental authority. Still, it was best not to take any chances.

The man's smile turned a bit mischievous.

"So what does your mother think about hitchhiking?" he asked.

April flushed with embarrassment.

"Oh, she's fine with it," she said.

The man chuckled. It wasn't a very pleasant sound. And something occurred to April. He'd asked what her *mother* thought, not what her *parents* thought. What made him say it that way?

The traffic was fairly heavy this close to the school at this time of morning. It was going to take a while to get home. April hoped that the man wasn't going to make a whole lot of conversation. That could get really awkward.

But after a couple of blocks of silence, April felt even more uncomfortable. The man had stopped smiling, and his expression seemed rather grim to her. She noticed that all the doors were locked. She surreptitiously fingered the button of the passenger-side window. It didn't budge.

The car came to a stop behind a line of cars waiting for a light to change. The man clicked on the left turn signal. April was seized by a sudden burst of anxiety.

"Um … we have to go straight here," she said.

The man said nothing. Had he simply not heard her? Somehow, she couldn't get up the nerve to say it again. Besides, maybe he planned to go by a different route. But no, she couldn't think of how he could drive her home from that direction.

April wondered what to do. Should she scream for help? Would anybody hear her? And what if the man hadn't heard what she said? Didn't mean any harm after all? The whole thing would be horribly embarrassing.

Then she saw someone familiar slouching along the sidewalk, his backpack slung over his shoulder. It was Brian, her sort-of-boyfriend these days. She rapped sharply on the window.

She gasped with relief when Brian looked around and saw her.

"Do you want a ride?" she mouthed to Brian.

Brian grinned and nodded.

"Oh, that's my boyfriend," April said. "Could we stop and pick him up, please? He's on his way to my house anyway."

It was a lie. April really had no idea where Brian was headed. The man scowled and grunted. He wasn't at all happy with this. Was he going to stop? April's heart beat wildly.

Brian was talking on his cell phone as he stood on the sidewalk and waited. But he was looking straight at the car and April was sure that he could see the driver pretty clearly. She was glad to have a potential witness just in case the man had something ugly in mind.

The man studied Brian, and he clearly saw him talking on his cell, and saw him looking back right at him.

Without saying a word, the man unlocked the doors. April

19

signaled for Brian to get in the back seat, so he opened the door and jumped in. He shut the door just as the light changed and the line of cars started to move again.

"Thanks for the ride, mister," Brian said brightly.

The man didn't say anything at all. He kept on scowling.

"He's taking us to my house, Brian," April said.

"Awesome," Brian replied.

April felt safe now. If the man really had bad intentions, he surely wasn't going to snatch both her and Brian. He'd surely drive them straight to Mom's house.

Thinking ahead, April wondered whether she should tell her mother about the man and her suspicions about him. But no, that would mean admitting to skipping her class and hitchhiking. Mom would ground her for good.

Besides, she thought, the driver couldn't be Peterson.

Peterson was a psychotic killer, not a regular man driving a car.

And Peterson, after all, was dead.

Chapter 5

Brent Meredith's tight, grim expression told Riley that he didn't like her request at all.

"It's an obvious case for me to take," she said. "I have more experience than anybody else with this kind of kinky serial killer."

She had just described the call from Reedsport, Meredith's jaw set the entire time.

After a long silence, Meredith finally sighed.

"I'll allow it," he said reluctantly.

Riley breathed a sigh of relief.

"Thank you, sir," she said.

"Don't thank me," he growled. "I'm doing this against my better judgment. I'm only going along with it because you've got the special skills to deal with this case. Your experience with this kind of killer is unique. I'll assign you a partner."

Riley felt a jolt of discouragement. She knew that working with Bill wasn't an option right now, but she wondered if Meredith knew why there was tension between the long-time partners. She thought it more likely that Bill had simply told Meredith that he wanted to stay close to home for now.

"But sir—" she began.

"No buts," Meredith said. "And no more of your lone wolf shenanigans. It's not smart, and it's against policy. You've nearly gotten yourself killed more than once. Rules are rules. And I'm breaking enough of them right now as it is, not putting you on leave after your recent incidents."

"Yes, sir," Riley said quietly.

Meredith rubbed his chin, obviously considering all the options. He said, "Agent Vargas will go with you."

"Lucy Vargas?" Riley asked.

Meredith just nodded. Riley didn't much like the idea.

"She was on the team that showed up at my house last night," Riley said. "She seems very impressive, and I liked her—but she's a rookie. I'm used to working with someone more experienced."

Meredith smiled broadly. "Her marks at the academy were off the charts. And she's young, all right. It's rare that students right out of the academy get accepted to BAU. But she really is that good. She's ready for experience in the field."

Riley knew she had no choice.

Meredith continued, "How soon can you be ready to go?"

Riley ran the necessary preparations through her mind. Talking to her daughter was at the top of her list. And what else? Her travel kit wasn't here in her office. She'd have to drive to Fredericksburg, stop at home, then make sure that April would stay at her father's and drive back to Quantico.

"Give me three hours," she said.

"I'll call for a plane," Meredith said. "I'll notify the police chief in Reedsport that we have a team on the way. Be at the airstrip in exactly three hours. If you're late, there'll be hell to pay."

Riley rose nervously from her chair.

"I understand, sir," she said. She almost thanked him again, but hastily remembered his command not to. She left his office without another word.

*

Riley made it to her house in half an hour, parked outside, and made a beeline for the front door. She had to grab her travel kit, a small suitcase she always kept packed with toiletries, a robe, and a change of clothes. She had to get them super fast and then go into town, where she'd explain things to April and Ryan. She wasn't looking forward to that part at all, but she needed to be sure that April was safe.

When she turned the key in the front door, she found that it was already unlocked. She knew she had locked it when she left. She always did, without fail. All of Riley's senses snapped into alertness. She pulled out her gun and stepped inside.

As she moved stealthily into the house, peering around at every nook and corner, she became aware of a long, continuous noise. It seemed to be coming from outside the house, in back. It was music—very loud music.

What the hell?

Still on the lookout for any intruder, she went through the kitchen. The back door was partly open and a pop song was blaring outside. She smelled a familiar aroma.

"Oh, Jesus, not this again," she said to herself.

She put her gun back into its holster and walked outside. Sure enough, there was April, sitting at the picnic table with a skinny boy about her age. The music was coming from a pair of little speakers sitting on the picnic table.

Upon seeing her mother, April's eyes lit up with panic. She reached under the picnic table to extinguish the joint in her hand, obviously hoping to make it disappear.

22

"Don't bother to hide it," Riley said, striding toward the table. "I know what you're doing."

She could barely make herself heard over the music. She reached over to the player and turned it off.

"This isn't what it looks like, Mom," April said.

"This is *exactly* what it looks like," Riley said. "Give me the rest of it."

Rolling her eyes, April handed over a plastic bag with a small amount of pot in it.

"I thought you were working," April said, as if that explained everything.

Riley didn't know whether to feel more angry or disappointed. She'd caught April smoking pot just once before. But things had gotten better between them, and she'd thought those days were behind them.

Riley stared at the boy.

"Mom, this is Brian," April said. "He's a friend from school."

With a vacant grin and glassy eyes, the boy reached out to shake hands with Riley.

"Pleased to meet you, Ms. Paige," he said.

Riley kept her own hands at her sides.

"What are you even doing here?" Riley asked April.

"This is where I live," April said with a shrug.

"You know what I mean. You're supposed to be at your dad's house."

April didn't reply. Riley looked at her watch. Time was running short. She had to resolve this situation quickly.

"Tell me what happened," Riley said.

April was starting to look somewhat embarrassed. She really wasn't prepared for this situation.

"I walked to school from Dad's house this morning," she said. "I ran into Brian in front of the school. We decided to skip today. It's okay if I miss it once in a while. I'm acing it already. The final exam isn't till Friday."

Brian let out a nervous, inane laugh.

"Yeah, April really is doing great in that class, Ms. Paige," he said. "She's awesome."

"How did you get here?" Riley asked.

April looked away. Riley easily guessed why she was reluctant to tell her the truth.

"Oh, God, you kids hitchhiked here, didn't you?" Riley said.

"The driver was a really nice guy, very quiet," April said.

"Brian was with me the whole time. We were safe."

Riley struggled to keep her nerves and her voice steady.

"How do you *know* you were safe? April, you're *never* supposed to accept rides from strangers. And why would you come here after the scare we got last night? That was incredibly foolish. Suppose Peterson was still around?"

April smiled as if she knew better.

"C'mon, Mom. You worry too much. The other agents say so. I heard two of them talking about it—the guys who drove me to Dad's house last night. They said Peterson was definitely dead, and you just couldn't accept it. They said whoever left those stones probably did it as a prank."

Riley was steaming. She wished she could get her hands on those agents. They had a lot of nerve, contradicting Riley within earshot of her daughter. She thought about asking April for their names, but she decided to let that go.

"Listen to me, April," Riley said. "I've got to go out of town on a job for a few days. I have to leave right now. I'm taking you to your Dad's house. I need for you to stay there."

"Why can't I go with you?" April asked.

Riley wondered how on earth teenage kids could be so stupid about some things.

"Because you've got to finish this class," she said. "You've got to pass it or you'll be behind in school. English is a requirement, and you blew it for no good reason. And besides, I'm working. Being around while I'm on the job isn't always safe. You ought to know that by now."

April said nothing.

"Come on inside," Riley said. "We've only got a few minutes. I've got to get some things together, and so do you. Then I'm taking you to your father's house."

Turning to Brian, Riley added, "And I'm driving you home."

"I can hitch," Brian said.

Riley simply glared at him.

"Okay," Brian said, looking rather cowed. He and April got up from the table and followed Riley into the house.

"Go on and get in the car, both of you," she said. The kids obediently left the house.

She latched the new slide bolt that she'd added to the back door and went from room to room making sure that all the windows were fastened.

In her own bedroom, she picked up her travel bag and made

24

sure that everything she needed was still inside. As she left, she glanced nervously at her bed as though the pebbles might have returned. For a moment, she wondered why she was headed off to another state instead of staying here and trying to track the killer who had put them there to taunt her.

Besides, this stunt of April's had her scared. Could she trust her daughter to stay safe in Fredericksburg? She'd thought so before, but now she had her doubts.

Still, there wasn't anything she could do to change things. She was committed to the new case and had to leave. As she walked outside to the car, she glanced into the thick, dark woods, scanning them for any sign of Peterson.

But there was none.

Chapter 6

Riley glanced at her car clock as she drove the kids into an upscale part of Fredericksburg and shuddered to see how little time she had left. Meredith's words came rushing back.

If you're late, there'll be hell to pay.

Maybe—just maybe—she'd get to the airstrip on time. She had planned to just stop at home and grab a bag, and now things were getting a lot more complicated. She wondered if she should she call Meredith and warn him that family problems might hold her up. No, she decided; her boss had been reluctant enough as it was. She couldn't expect him to cut her any slack.

Luckily, Brian's address was on the route to Ryan's house. When Riley pulled up to a big front yard and stopped the car, she said, "I ought to come in and tell your parents what happened."

"They're not at home," Brian said with a shrug. "Dad's gone for good, and Mom isn't there much."

He got out of the car, then turned and said, "Thanks for the ride." As he walked toward his house Riley wondered what kind of parents would leave a kid like that on his own. Didn't they know what kind of trouble a teenager could get into?

But maybe his mother doesn't have much choice in that matter, Riley thought miserably. *Who am I to judge?*

As soon as Brian went inside his house, Riley drove away. April had said nothing during the whole drive so far, and she didn't seem to be in any mood to talk now. Riley couldn't tell whether that silence was due to sullenness or shame. She realized that there seemed to be a lot she didn't know about her own daughter.

Riley was upset with both herself and April. Just yesterday they'd seemed to be getting along better. She'd thought that April was beginning to understand the pressures on an FBI agent. But then Riley had insisted that April go to her father's house last night, and today April was rebelling against being forced to do that.

Riley reminded herself that she ought to be a whole lot more sympathetic. She'd always been something of a rebel herself. And Riley knew what it was like to lose a mother and to have a distant father. April was bound to be afraid that the same thing would happen to her.

She's terrified for my safety, Riley realized. During recent months, April had seen her mother endure both physical and emotional injuries. After last night's intruder scare, April was surely worried sick. Riley reminded herself that she needed to pay closer attention to how her daughter might be feeling. Anyone of any age might have a hard time coping with the complications of Riley's life.

Riley pulled in front of the house she had once shared with Ryan. It was a large, handsome house with a portico at the side door, or *porte-cochère* as Ryan called it. These days, Riley chose to park on the street instead of pulling into the driveway and under the shelter.

She had never felt at home here. Somehow, living in a respectable suburban neighborhood had never suited her. Her marriage, the house, the neighborhood, all had represented so many expectations that she'd never felt able to fulfill.

Over the years Riley had realized that she was better at her job than she would ever be at living a normal life. Finally she had left the marriage, house, and neighborhood, and that made her all the more determined to live up to the expectations of being a mother to a teenage daughter.

As April started to open the car door, Riley said, "Wait."

April turned and looked at her expectantly.

Without so much as stopping to think, Riley said, "I get it. I understand."

April stared at her with a stunned expression. For a moment, she seemed on the verge of tears. Riley felt almost as surprised as her daughter. She didn't know quite what had come over her. She only knew that now was no time for parental lectures, even if she had time to deliver one, which she didn't. She also felt in her gut that she'd said exactly the right thing.

Riley and April got out of the car and walked together to the house. She didn't know whether to hope Ryan would be at home or not. She didn't want to get into an argument with him, and she'd already decided not to tell him about the marijuana incident. She knew she ought to, but there simply wasn't time to deal with his reactions. Still, she really did have to explain to him that she was going to be gone for a few days.

Gabriela, the stout, middle-aged Guatemalan woman who had worked as the family's housekeeper for years, greeted Riley and April at the door. Gabriela's eyes were wide with worry.

"*Hija*, where have you been?" she asked in her heavy accent.

"I'm sorry, Gabriela," April said meekly.

Gabriela looked closely at April's face. Riley saw by her expression that she detected that April had been smoking pot.

"*Tonta!*" Gabriela said sharply.

"*Lo siento mucho,*" April said, sounding genuinely repentant.

"*Vente conmigo,*" Gabriela said. As she led April away, she turned and gave Riley a look of bitter disapproval.

Riley withered under that look. Gabriela was one of the few people in the world who truly daunted her. The woman also had a wonderful way with April, and at the moment, she seemed to be doing a better job of parenting than Riley was.

Riley called after Gabriela, "Is Ryan here?"

As she walked away, Gabriela replied, "*Sí.*" Then she called into the house, "Señor Paige, your daughter is back."

Ryan appeared in the hallway, dressed and coiffed to leave. He looked surprised to see Riley.

"What are you doing here?" he asked. "Where was April?"

"She was at my house."

"What? After everything that happened last night, you took her home?"

Riley's jaw clenched with exasperation.

"I didn't take her anywhere," she said. "Ask her, if you want to know how she got there. I can't help it if she doesn't want to live with you. You're the only one who can fix that."

"This is all your fault, Riley. You've let her get completely out of control."

For a split second, Riley was furious. But her fury gave way to a sinking feeling that he might be right. It wasn't fair, but he really did know how to push her buttons that way.

Riley took a long, deep breath and said, "Look, I'm leaving town for a few days. I've got a case in Upstate New York. April has got to stay here, and she's got to stay put. Please explain the situation to Gabriela."

"*You* explain the situation to Gabriela," Ryan snapped. "I've got a client to meet. Right now."

"And I've got a plane to catch. Right now."

They stood staring at each other for a moment. Their argument had reached a stalemate. As she looked into his eyes, Riley reminded herself that she'd once loved him. And he'd seemed to love her just as much. That had been back when both of them were young and poor, before he had become a successful lawyer and she had become an FBI agent.

She couldn't help noting that he was still a very good-looking man. He went to a lot of trouble to look that way and spent many hours at the gym. Riley also knew perfectly well that he had lots of women in his life. That was part of the problem—he was enjoying

28

his freedom as a bachelor too much to worry about parenting.

Not that I'm doing all that much better, she thought.

Then Ryan said, "It's always about your job."

Riley choked back her anger. They'd gone around and around about this. Her job was somehow both too dangerous and too trivial. His job was all that mattered, because he was making a lot more money, and because he claimed to be making a real difference in the world. As if handling lawsuits for wealthy clients amounted to more than Riley's never-ending war against evil.

But she couldn't let herself get dragged into this tired old argument right now. Neither of them ever won it anyway.

"We'll talk when I get back," she said.

She turned and walked out of the house. She heard Ryan shut the door behind her.

Riley got into her car and drove. She had less than an hour to get back to Quantico. Her head was reeling. So much was happening so fast. Just a little while ago she had decided to take a new case. Now she wondered if it was the right thing to do. Not only was April having trouble coping, but she was sure that Peterson was back in her life.

But in a way, it made good sense. As long as April stayed with her father, she'd be safe from Peterson's clutches. And Peterson wasn't going to take any other victims during Riley's absence. As puzzled as she was by him, Riley knew one thing for certain. She alone was his target for revenge. She, and no one else, was his intended next victim. And it would feel good to be far away from him for a while.

She also reminded herself of a hard lesson she had learned during her last case—not to take on all the evil in the world, all at the same time. It boiled down to a simple motto: *One monster at a time.*

And right now, she was going after an especially vicious brute. A man she just knew would strike again soon.

29

Chapter 7

The man began to spread lengths of chains out on the long worktable in his basement. It was dark outside, but all those links of stainless steel were bright and shiny under the glare of a bare light bulb.

He pulled one of the chains out to its full length. The rattling sound stirred terrible memories of being shackled, caged, and tormented with chains like these. But it was like he kept telling himself: *I've got to face my fears.*

And to do that he had to prove his mastery over the chains themselves. Too often in the past, chains had held mastery over him.

It was a shame that anyone had to suffer on account of this. For five years, he'd thought he'd put the whole matter behind him. It had helped so much when the church hired him to be a night watchman. He'd liked that job, proud of the authority that came with it. He'd liked feeling strong and useful.

But last month, they'd taken that job away from him. They needed someone with security skills, they'd said, and better credentials—someone bigger and stronger. They promised to keep him working in the garden. He'd still be making enough money to pay the rent on this tiny little house.

Even so, the loss of that job, the loss of the authority it gave him, had shaken him, made him feel helpless. That urge broke loose again—that desperation not to be helpless, that frantic need to assert mastery over the chains so they couldn't take him again. He'd tried before to outrun the urge, as if he could leave his inner darkness right here in his basement. This last time, he'd driven all the way down to Reedsport, hoping to escape it. But he couldn't.

He didn't know why he couldn't. He was a good man, with a good heart, and he liked to do favors. But sooner or later, his kindness always turned against him. When he'd helped that woman, that nurse, carry groceries to her car in Reedsport, she'd smiled and said, "What a good boy!"

He winced at the memory of the smile and those words.

"What a good boy!"

His mother had smiled and said such things, even while she kept the chain on his leg too short for him to reach any food or even see outside. And the nuns, too, had smiled and said things like that when they peered at him through the little square opening in the door to his small prison.

30

"What a good boy!"

Not everyone was cruel, he knew that. Most people really meant well toward him, especially in this little town where he'd long since settled. They even liked him. But why did everyone seem to think of him as a child—and a handicapped child at that? He was twenty-seven years old, and he knew that he was exceptionally bright. His mind was full of brilliant thoughts, and he scarcely ever encountered a problem he couldn't solve.

But of course he knew why people saw him the way they did. It was because he could barely speak at all. He'd stammered hopelessly all his life, and he hardly ever tried to talk, although he understood everything that other people said.

And he was small, and weak, and his features were stubby and childish, like those of someone who had been born with some congenital defect. Caged in that slightly misshapen skull was a remarkable mind, thwarted in its desire to do brilliant things in the world. But nobody knew that. Nobody at all. Not even the doctors at the psychiatric hospital had known it.

It was *ironic.*

People didn't think he knew words like *ironic.* But he did.

Now he found himself nervously fingering a button in his hand. He'd plucked it off the nurse's blouse when he hung her up. Reminded of her, he looked around at the cot where he'd kept her chained up for more than a week. He'd wished he could talk to her, explain that he didn't mean to be cruel, and it was just that she was so much like his mother and the nuns, especially in that nurse's uniform of hers.

The sight of her in that uniform had confused him. It was the same with the woman five years ago, the prison guard. Somehow both women had merged in his mind with his mother and the nuns and the hospital workers. He'd fought a losing battle simply to tell them apart.

It was a relief to be through with her. It was a terrible responsibility, keeping her bound like that, giving her water, listening to her moaning through the chain he'd used to gag her. He only undid the gag to put a straw in her mouth for water now and again. Then she'd try to scream.

If only he could have explained to her that she *mustn't* scream, that there were neighbors across the street who mustn't hear. If he could only have told her, maybe she'd have understood. But he couldn't explain, not with his hopeless stammer. Instead, he'd mutely threatened her with a straight-edged razor. In the long run, even the threat hadn't worked. That was when he'd had to slit her throat.

Then he'd taken her back to Reedsport and hung her up like that, for everyone to see. He wasn't sure just why. Perhaps it was a warning. If only people could understand. If they did, he wouldn't have to be so cruel.

Perhaps it was also his way of telling the world how sorry he was.

Because he *was* sorry. He'd go to the florist tomorrow and buy flowers—a cheap little bouquet—for the family. He couldn't talk to the florist, but he could write out simple instructions. The gift would be anonymous. And if he could find a good place to hide, he'd stand near the grave when they buried her, bowing his head like any other mourner.

He pulled another chain taut on his workbench, clenching its ends as tightly as he could, applying all his strength to it, silencing its rattle. But deep down, he knew that this wasn't enough to make him master of the chains. For that, he'd have to put the chains to use again. And he'd use one of the straitjackets still in his possession. Someone must be bound, as he'd been bound.

Someone else would have to suffer and die.

Chapter 8

As soon as Riley and Lucy stepped off the FBI plane, a young uniformed cop came dashing toward them across the tarmac.

"Boy, am I glad to see you guys," he said. "Chief Alford's fit to be tied. If somebody doesn't take Rosemary's body down directly, he's liable to have a stroke. Reporters are already all over this. I'm Tim Boyden."

Riley's heart sank as she and Lucy introduced themselves. Media on the scene so quickly was a sure sign of trouble. The case was off to a rocky start.

"Can I help you carry anything?" Officer Boyden asked.

"We're good," Riley said. She and Lucy had only a couple of small bags.

Officer Boyden pointed across the tarmac.

"The car's right over there," he said.

The three of them walked briskly to the car. Riley got in on the front passenger side, while Lucy took the back seat.

"We're just a couple of minutes from town," Boyden said as he started to drive. "Man, I can't believe this is happening. Poor Rosemary. Everybody liked her so much. She was always helping people. When she disappeared a couple of weeks ago, we were all scared for the worst. But we couldn't have imagined …"

His voice trailed off and he shook his head in horrified disbelief.

Lucy leaned forward from the back seat.

"I understand that you had a murder like this before," she said.

"Yeah, back when I was still in high school," Boyden said. "Not right here in Reedsport, though. It was near Eubanks, farther south along the river. A body in chains, just like Rosemary. Wearing a straitjacket too. Is the chief right? Do we have a serial on our hands?"

"We're not ready to say," Riley said.

The truth was, she thought that the chief must be right. But the young officer seemed upset enough already. There seemed no point in alarming him further.

"I can't believe it," Boyden said, shaking his head again. "A nice little town like ours. A nice lady like Rosemary. I can't believe it."

As they drove into town, Riley saw a couple of vans with TV news crews on its little main street. A helicopter with a TV station logo was circling above the town.

Boyden drove to a barricade where a small cluster of reporters had gathered. An officer waved the car on through. Just a few seconds later, Boyden pulled the car alongside a stretch of railroad track. There was the body, hanging from a power pole. Several uniformed policemen were standing a few yards away from it.

As Riley stepped out of the car, she recognized Chief Raymond Alford as he trotted toward her. He looked none too happy.

"I sure as hell hope you had a good reason for us keeping the body hanging here like this," he said. "We've had a nightmare on our hands. The mayor's threatening to take my badge."

Riley and Lucy followed him toward the body. In the late afternoon sunlight, it looked even weirder than it had in the photos Riley had viewed on her computer. The stainless steel chains sparkled in the light.

"I take it you've cordoned off the scene," Riley said to Alford.

"We've done it as best we could," Alford said. "We've got the area barricaded far enough away that nobody can see the body except from the river. We've rerouted the trains to go around the town. It's slowing them down and playing havoc with their schedule. That must be how the Albany news channels found out that something was going on. They sure didn't hear about it from my people."

As Alford spoke, his voice was drowned out by the TV helicopter as it hovered directly overhead. He gave up trying to say what he meant to say. Riley could read the profanities on his lips as he looked up at the aircraft. Without rising, the helicopter swung away in a circle. The pilot obviously intended to circle back this way.

Alford took out his cell phone. When he got someone on the line, he yelled, "I *told* you to keep your damned chopper away from the site. Now tell your pilot to take that thing up above five hundred feet. It's the law."

From Alford's expression, Riley suspected that the person on the other end was giving him some resistance.

Finally Alford said, "If you don't get that bird out of here right now, your reporters are going to be barred from the news conference I'll be giving this afternoon."

His face relaxed a little. He looked up and waited. Sure enough, after a few moments the helicopter rose to a more reasonable height. The noise from its engine still filled the air with a loud and steady drone.

"God, I hope we don't get a lot more of this," Alford growled.

34

"Maybe when we cut the body down, there'll be less here to attract them. Still, in the short run, I guess there's an upside. The hotels and B&Bs are getting some extra business. Restaurants too— reporters have got to eat. But in the long run? It's bad if tourists get scared off from Reedsport."

"You've done a good job keeping them away from the scene," Riley said.

"I guess that's something," Alford said. "Come on, let's get this over with."

Alford led Riley and Lucy nearer to the suspended body. The body was held in a makeshift chain harness that wrapped around and around it. The harness was tied to a heavy rope that looped through a steel pulley attached to a high crossbeam. The rest of the rope descended to the ground at a sharp angle.

Riley could see the woman's face now. Once again, her resemblance to Marie shot through her like an electric shock—the same silent pain and anguish that her friend's face had displayed after she'd hanged herself. The bulging eyes and the chain that gagged the mouth made the sight all the more disturbing.

Riley looked at her new partner to see how she was reacting. Somewhat to her surprise, she saw that Lucy was already taking notes.

"Is this your first murder scene?" Riley asked her.

Lucy simply nodded while she wrote and observed. Riley thought she was taking the sight of the corpse awfully well. A lot of rookies would be off vomiting in the bushes at this point.

By contrast, Alford looked decidedly queasy. Even after all these hours, he hadn't gotten used to it. For his sake, Riley hoped that he'd never need to.

"Not much of a smell yet," Alford said.

"Not yet," Riley said. "She's still in a state of autolysis, mostly just internal cell breakdown. It's not hot enough to speed the putrefaction process along. The body hasn't started melting down from the inside. That's when the smell would get really bad."

Alford looked more and more pale at this kind of talk.

"What about rigor mortis?" Lucy asked.

"She's in full rigor, I'm sure," Riley said. "She probably will be for another twelve hours."

Lucy still didn't look the least bit fazed. She just kept jotting down more notes.

"Have you figured out how the killer got her up there?" Lucy asked Alford.

"We've got a pretty good idea," Alford said. "He climbed up and tied the pulley in place. Then he hauled the body up. You can see how it's anchored."

Alford pointed to a bundle of iron weights lying next to the tracks. The rope was tied through holes in the weights, knotted carefully so that it wouldn't come loose. The weights were the kind that might be found in weight machines at a gym.

Lucy bent down and looked at the weights more closely.

"There's almost enough weight here to completely counterbalance the body," Lucy said. "Odd that he dragged all this heavy stuff with him. You'd think he'd have just tied the rope directly to the pole."

"What does that tell you?" Riley asked.

Lucy thought for a moment.

"He's small and not very strong," Lucy said. "The pulley didn't give him enough leverage by itself. He needed the weights to help him."

"Very good," Riley said. Then she pointed to the opposite side of the train tracks. For a brief stretch, a partial tire track veered off the nearby pavement onto to the dirt. "And you can see that he pulled his vehicle up very close. He had to. He couldn't drag the body very far on his own."

Riley examined the ground near the power pole and found sharp indentations in the earth.

"It looks like he used a ladder," she said.

"Yeah, and we found the ladder," Alford said. "Come on, I'll show you."

Alford led Riley and Lucy across the tracks to a weather-beaten warehouse made of corrugated steel. There was a broken lock hanging from the hasp of the door.

"You can see how he broke in here," Alford said. "It was easy enough to do. A pair of bolt cutters would have done the trick. This warehouse isn't used for much, just long-term storage, so it's not very secure."

Alford opened the door and switched on the fluorescent overhead lights. The place was, indeed, mostly empty, except for a few shipping crates swarming with cobwebs. Alford pointed to a tall ladder leaning against the wall next to the door.

"There's the ladder," he said. "We found fresh dirt on its feet. It probably belongs here, and the killer knew about it. He broke in, dragged it out, and climbed it to tie the pulley in place. Once he got the body where he wanted it, he dragged the ladder back here. Then he drove off."

"Maybe he got the pulley from inside the warehouse too," Lucy suggested.

"The front of this warehouse is lit up at night," Alford said. "So he's bold, and I'll bet he's pretty fast, even if he isn't very strong."

At that moment there came a sharp, loud crack outside.

"What the hell?" Alford yelled.

Riley knew immediately that it was a gunshot.

Chapter 9

Alford drew his gun and charged out of the warehouse. Riley and Lucy followed with their hands on their own weapons. Outside, something was hovering in circles around the pole where the body was hanging. It made a steady buzzing sound.

Young Officer Boyden had his pistol drawn. He had just taken a shot at the small drone that was circling the body and was getting ready to take another.

"Boyden, put that damned gun away!" Alford shouted. He holstered his own weapon.

Boyden turned toward Alford with surprise. Just as he was putting away his weapon, the drone rose higher and flew away.

The chief was fuming.

"What the hell did you think you were doing, firing your weapon like that?" he snarled at Boyden.

"Protecting the scene," Boyden said. "It's probably some blogger taking pictures."

"Probably," Alford said. "And I don't like that any more than you do. But it's illegal to shoot those things down. Besides, this is a populated area. You ought to know better."

Boyden hung his head sheepishly.

"Sorry, sir," he said.

Alford turned toward Riley.

"Drones, hell!" he said. "I sure do hate the twenty-first century. Agent Paige, please tell me we can take that body down now."

"Have you got more pictures than the ones I saw?" Riley asked.

"Lots of them, showing every little detail," Alford said. "You can look at them in my office."

Riley nodded. "I've seen what I needed to see here. And you've done a good job keeping the scene under control. Go ahead and cut her down."

Alford said to Boyden, "Call the county coroner. Tell him he can stop waiting around twiddling his thumbs."

"Got it, Chief," Boyden said, taking out his cell phone.

"Come on," Alford said to Riley and Lucy. He led them to his police car. When they got in and were on their way, a cop waved the car past the barricade onto the main street.

Riley took careful note of the route. The killer would have brought his vehicle in and out along this same route that both Boyden and Alford used. There was no other way into the area between the warehouse and the train tracks. It seemed likely that someone would have seen the killer's vehicle, although they might not have thought it unusual.

The Reedsport Police Department was nothing more than a little brick storefront right on the town's main street. Alford, Riley, and Lucy went inside and sat down in the chief's office.

Alford placed a stack of folders on his desk.

"Here's everything we've got," he said. "The complete file on the old case from five years ago, and everything so far on last night's murder."

Riley and Lucy each took a folder and began to browse through it. Riley's attention was drawn to the photos of the first case.

The two women were similar in age. The first one worked in a prison, which put her at some degree of risk for possible victimization. But the second one would be considered a lower risk victim. And there was no indication that either of them frequented bars or other places that would make them especially vulnerable. In both cases, those who knew the women had described them as friendly, helpful, and conventional. And yet, there had to be some factor that drew the killer to these particular women.

"Did you make any headway on Marla Blainey's murder?" Riley asked Alford.

"It was under the jurisdiction of the Eubanks police. Captain Lawson. But I worked with him on it. We found out nothing useful. The chains were perfectly ordinary. The killer could have picked them up at any hardware store."

Lucy leaned toward Riley to look at the same pictures.

"Still, he did buy a lot of them," Lucy said. "You'd think some clerk would have noticed someone buying so many chains."

Alford nodded in agreement.

"Yeah, that's what we thought at the time. But we contacted hardware stores all around these parts. None of the clerks picked up on any unusual sales like that. He must have bought a few at a time, here and there, without attracting a lot of attention. By the time he got around to the murder, he had big pile of them handy. Maybe he still does."

Riley peered closely at the straitjacket the woman was wearing. It looked identical to the one used to bind last night's victim.

"What about the straitjacket?" Riley asked.

Alford shrugged. "You'd think something like that would be easy to track. But we got nothing. It's standard issue in psychiatric hospitals. We checked all the hospitals throughout the state, including one real close by. Nobody noticed any straitjackets missing or stolen."

A silence fell as Riley and Lucy continued looking at reports and photos. The bodies had been left within ten miles of each other. That indicated that the killer probably didn't live too far away. But the first woman's corpse had been dumped unceremoniously on a riverbank. Over the five years between murders, the killer's attitude had changed in some way.

"So what do you make of this guy?" Alford asked. "Why the straitjacket and all the chains? Doesn't that seem like overkill?"

Riley thought for a moment.

"Not in his mind," she said. "It's about power. He wants to restrict his victims not just physically but symbolically. It goes way beyond the practical. It's about taking away the victim's power. The killer wants to make a real point of that."

"But why women?" Lucy asked. "If he wants to disempower his victims, wouldn't it be more dramatic with men?"

"It's a good question," Riley replied. She thought back to the crime scene—how the body had been so carefully counterbalanced.

"But remember, he's not very strong," Riley said. "It might be partly a matter of choosing easier targets. Middle-aged women like these would probably put up less of a fight. But they also probably stand for something in his mind. They weren't selected as individuals, but as *women*—and whatever it is that women represent to him."

Alford let out a cynical growl.

"So you're saying it was nothing personal," he said. "It's not like these women *did* anything to get captured and killed. It's not like the killer even thought they especially deserved it."

"That's often how it goes," Riley said. "In my last case, the killer targeted women who bought dolls. He didn't care who they were. All that mattered is that he saw them buy a doll."

Another silence fell. Alford looked at his watch.

"I've got a press conference in about a half hour," he said. "Is there anything else we need to discuss before then?"

Riley said, "Well, the sooner Agent Vargas and I can interview the victim's immediate family, the better. This evening, if that's possible."

Alford knitted his brow with concern.

"I don't think so," he said. "Her husband died young, maybe fifteen years ago. All she's got is a couple of grown-up kids, a son and a daughter, both with families of their own. They live right in town. My people have been interviewing them all day. They're really worn out and distraught. Let's give them till tomorrow before we put them through any more of that."

Riley saw that Lucy was about to object, so she stopped her with a silent gesture. It was smart of Lucy to want to interview the family immediately. But Riley also knew better than to make waves with the local force, especially if they seemed to be as competent as Alford and his team.

"I understand," Riley said. "Let's try for tomorrow morning. What about the family of the first victim?"

"I think there might still be some relatives down in Eubanks," Alford said. "I'll check into it. Let's just not rush anything. The killer's in no hurry, after all. His last murder was five years ago, and he's not liable to act again soon. Let's take time to do things right."

Alford got up from his chair.

"I'd better get ready for the press conference," he said. "Do you two want to be part of it? Have you got any kind of statement to make?"

Riley mulled it over.

"No, I don't think so," she said. "It's best if the FBI keeps a low profile for the time being. We don't want the killer to feel like he's getting a lot of publicity. He might be more likely to show himself if he doesn't think he's getting the attention he deserves. Right now, it's better for you to be the face people see."

"Well then, you can get settled in," Alford said. "I've got a couple of rooms at a local B&B reserved for you. There's also a car out front you can use."

He slid the room reservation form and a set of car keys across his desk to Riley. She and Lucy left the station.

*

Later that evening, Riley sat on a bay window seat looking out over Reedsport's main street. Dusk had fallen, and streetlights were coming on. The night air was warm and pleasant and all was quiet, with no reporters in sight.

Alford had reserved two lovely second-story rooms in the B&B for Riley and Lucy. The woman who owned the place had served a delicious supper. Then Riley and Lucy had spent an hour or so in the main room downstairs making plans for tomorrow.

Reedsport truly was a quaint and lovely town. Under different circumstances, it would be nice place for a vacation. But now that

41

Riley was away from all talk of yesterday's murder, her mind turned toward more familiar concerns.

She hadn't thought about Peterson all day until now. He was out there, and she knew it, but nobody else believed it. Had she been wise to leave things like that? Should she have tried harder to convince somebody?

It gave her a chill to think that two murderers—Peterson and whoever had killed two women here—were at this very moment going about their lives however they pleased. How many more were out there, somewhere in the state, somewhere in the country? Why was our culture plagued with these warped human beings?

What might they be doing? Were they plotting somewhere in isolation, or were they comfortably passing their time with friends and family—unsuspecting, innocent people who had no idea of the evil in their midst?

At the moment, Riley had no way to know. But it was her job to find out.

She also found herself thinking anxiously about April. It hadn't felt right to simply leave her with her father. But what else was she to do? Riley knew that even if she had not taken this case, another one would come along soon. She was simply too involved in her work to deal with an unruly teenager. She wasn't home enough.

On an impulse, Riley took out her cell phone and sent a text message.

Hey April. How are U?

After a few seconds, the reply came.

I'm fine Mom. How are U? Have U solved it yet?

It took Riley a moment to realize that April meant the new case.

Not yet, she typed.

April replied, *U'll solve it soon.*

Riley smiled at what sounded almost like a vote of confidence.

She typed, *Do U want to talk? I could call U now.*

She waited a few moments for April's reply.

Not right now. I'm good.

Riley didn't know exactly what that meant. Her heart sank a little.

OK, she typed. *Goodnight. Love U.*

She ended the chat and sat there, looking out into the deepening night. She smiled wistfully as she remembered April's question …

"Have U solved it yet?"

"It" could mean any of a huge number of things in Riley's life.

42

And she felt a long, long way from solving any of them.

Riley stared out into the night again. Looking down at the main street, she pictured the killer driving straight through town on the way to the railroad tracks. It had been a bold move. But not nearly as bold as taking the time to hang the body from a power pole where it would be visible in the light from the warehouse.

That part of his MO had changed drastically over the last five years, from sloppily dumping a body by the river to hanging this one up for the world to see. He didn't strike Riley as particularly organized, but he was becoming more obsessive. Something in his life must have changed. What was it?

Riley knew that this kind of boldness often represented an escalating desire for publicity, for fame. That was certainly true of the last killer she had tracked down. But it felt wrong for this case. Something told Riley that this killer was not only small and rather weak, but also self-effacing, even humble.

He didn't like to kill; Riley felt pretty sure of it. And it wasn't fame that spurred him to this new level of boldness. It was sheer despair. Perhaps even remorse, a half-conscious desire to get caught.

Riley knew from personal experience that killers were never more dangerous than when they started turning against themselves.

Riley thought about something Chief Alford had said earlier.

"The killer's in no hurry, after all."

Riley felt sure that the chief was wrong.

43

Chapter 10

Riley felt sorry for the county coroner, a middle-aged and overweight man, as he spread out the photos on Chief Alford's desk. They displayed every gruesome detail of Rosemary Pickens's autopsy. The coroner, Ben Tooley, looked slightly ill. He was undoubtedly more accustomed to examining corpses of people who had died from strokes and heart attacks. He looked as he if he hadn't slept, and she realized he'd surely been up late last night. And Riley guessed that he hadn't slept soundly whenever he had gotten to bed.

It was morning, and Riley felt remarkably rested herself. Her bed had been soft and comfortable, and neither nightmares nor real intruders had disturbed her sleep. She had badly needed a night like that. Lucy and Chief Alford also looked alert—but the coroner was another story.

"This is as bad as Marla Blainey's murder five years ago," Tooley said. "Worse, maybe. Lord, after that one, I'd hoped we'd put this kind of awful thing behind us. No such luck."

Tooley showed the group a close-up of the back of the woman's head. A large, deep wound was visible, and the surrounding hair was matted with blood.

"She sustained a sharp blow to the left parietal bone," he said. "It was hard enough to crack the skull slightly. Probably caused concussion, maybe even a short interval of unconsciousness."

"What kind of object was used?" Riley asked.

"Judging from the pulled hair and scraping, I'd say it was a blow from a heavy chain. Marla Blainey had the same kind of wound in about the same place."

Alford shook his head. "This guy is all about chains," he said. "Reporters are already calling him the 'chain killer.'"

Lucy pointed to some tight close-ups of the woman's abdomen.

"Do you think she was beaten generally, over time?" she asked. "Those bruises look bad."

"They're bad, all right, but they're not from being beaten," Tooley said. "She's got contusions like that all over from being chained so tightly. Between the chains and how tight the straitjacket was, she spent a lot of time in severe pain. Same with Marla Blainey."

The group fell silent for a moment, mulling over the significance of this information.

Finally Lucy said, "We know that he's small and not very

strong—and we're assuming that it really is a 'he.' So it looks like he must've subdued each of the women with a single sharp blow to the head. When they were dazed or unconscious, he lugged them into a nearby vehicle."

Riley nodded with approval. It struck her as a good guess.

"So how was she treated during her captivity?" Alford asked.

Tooley shuffled the photos to reveal images of the dissected body.

"Pretty badly," he said. "I found almost no stomach contents. Not much in her intestines either. He must have kept her alive on water alone. But he probably wasn't trying to starve her to death. That would have taken much longer. Maybe he was just trying to weaken her. Again, it was the same with Marla Blainey. The slashed throats were the decisive and fatal blows."

Another silence fell. There was little left for anyone to say, but much to think about. Riley's head was abuzz with too many questions to ask. Why did the killer hold these women captive? The usual motives didn't apply here. He didn't torture or rape them. If he'd always intended to kill them, why had he taken his time about it? Did it take time for him to build up the will to do that?

Obviously, she thought, the killer was obsessed with rendering his victims helpless. That gave him some kind of satisfaction. He'd probably suffered similar helplessness himself, maybe in childhood. She also suspected that he'd starved the victims for other reasons than simply to weaken them. Had the killer been starved himself at one time or another?

Riley stifled a sigh. There were so many questions. There always were this early in a case. Meanwhile, there was a lot of work to do.

*

Two hours later, Riley was driving Alford's loaner car south along the Hudson River, with Lucy as a passenger. They were on their way to Eubanks, the town where Marla Blainey had lived and was murdered. They had just left Rosemary Pickens's house, where they had interviewed her two grown children.

Riley reviewed the meeting in her mind. It hadn't been very productive, and the distraught brother and sister hadn't offered any solid information. They had no idea why their mother, always a kindly and helpful soul, would be targeted for such a brutal crime.

Still, Riley was now glad that she had left much of the

45

questioning to Lucy. Again, she was impressed by her new partner's work—especially her ability to deal with people who were undergoing terrible shock and grief. Lucy had gently gotten the brother and sister to reminisce about their mother quite freely.

Courtesy of Lucy's sympathetic questions, a portrait of Rosemary Pickens was becoming clearer. She had been a loving, witty, and generous woman who would be badly missed by her family and everyone else in Reedsport. Riley knew how important it was to develop this kind of understanding of a murder victim. Lucy was definitely doing good work so far.

As Riley drove along the two-lane road that bordered the wide Hudson River, she realized that she still knew very little about the talented young agent who was sitting beside her. Right now Lucy appeared to be deep in thought, undoubtedly considering the meager facts they had so far.

"Tell me something about yourself, Lucy," Riley said.

"Like what?" Lucy asked, looking at Riley with surprise.

Riley shrugged. "Well, you're not married, I take it. Have you got a significant other?"

"Not at the moment," Lucy said.

"How about the future?"

Lucy thought quietly for a moment.

"I don't know, Riley," she said at last. "I guess I'm not one for long-term attachments. Whenever I try to imagine life with a husband and kids, my mind just goes blank. Believe me, that kind of attitude doesn't go down well with a Mexican-American family. Some of my brothers and sisters have already got kids. My parents expect the same from me. I'm afraid they're going to be disappointed. But what can I do?"

Lucy fell silent again. Then she said, "It's just that I already love this job so much. There's good work to be done. I want to give it everything I've got, make a real difference in the world. I don't see how I could make time for anything else—not even a relationship. Does that sound selfish?"

Riley smiled rather sadly.

"Not selfish at all," she said.

By contrast, Riley had to wonder about her own choices. She'd tried to have it all—a marriage, a family, a demanding job. Had that been selfish of her? If she'd started off with Lucy's priorities, might things be better?

But then I wouldn't have April, she thought. *And April ... April is worth the extra effort.* She loved her daughter dearly and hoped that she hadn't botched the job of raising her to be a genuinely good adult.

A moment later they pulled into Eubanks. The town was larger than Reedsport, but it still wasn't hard to find the modest but pleasant two-story house. Two men were sitting a swing chair on the front porch. They rose to their feet when Riley and Lucy got out of the car and walked toward the house. A stocky, uniformed man of about Riley's age stepped forward to greet them.

"I'm Dwight Slater, officer in charge here in Eubanks," he said.

Riley and Lucy introduced themselves. The other man was tall with a strong, friendly face.

"This is Craig Blainey, Marla's widower," Slater said.

Blainey greeted Riley and Lucy with a handshake.

"Sit down, make yourselves comfortable," he said in a startlingly deep and pleasant voice. It occurred to Riley that he might make a good preacher.

Slater and Blainey sat back down on the swing chair, and Riley and Lucy sat in a pair of outdoor chairs facing it.

Riley began with the essentials.

"Mr. Blainey, it may seem strange for me to say so at this late date, but I'm very sorry for your loss. And I'm also sorry to have to dredge up what must be terrible memories. My partner and I will try to keep this short."

Blainey nodded.

"I appreciate that," he said. "But you should take as much time as you need. I understand there's been a new murder up in Reedsport. I'm very sorry to hear it. But if I can do or say anything to put a stop to this monster, it will do my heart good."

Riley took out a notepad and began to write. She noticed that Lucy did the same.

"What kind of work do you do, Mr. Blainey?" she asked.

"I own a hardware store. It's been in my family for a couple of generations. That tradition's coming to an end with me, though." His smile turned a bit melancholy. "My kids aren't interested in keeping the family business going. Not that I can complain, they're doing fine on their own. Jill's studying at the University of Buffalo and Alex is a radio announcer over on Long Island."

A note of pride had come into his voice.

Riley nodded to Lucy, a silent signal to go ahead and ask her own questions.

"Do you have any other family here in Eubanks?" Lucy asked.

"My brother and sister used to live here, and they've got kids

47

of their own. But the whole thing with Marla …"

Blainey paused for a moment to control a surge of emotion.

"Well, this town was never the same for them after that. The memory was just too awful. They had to get away. Amy and her family resettled in Philadelphia, and Baxter and his family moved up to Maine."

Blainey shrugged and shook his head.

"Don't know why I didn't feel the same way. I just felt all the more rooted here, for some reason. But then, I'm the type to remember the good times more than the bad. And Marla and I had a lot of good times here."

Blainey looked off into space with a wistful expression, lost for a moment in memories. Lucy spoke gently to bring him back to the present.

"I understand that your wife was a corrections officer," she said.

"That's right. In the men's penitentiary across the river."

Riley could see that Lucy was thinking hard about how to pose her next question as delicately as possible.

"Mr. Blainey, being a prison guard's a tough job, even for a man," Lucy said. "For a woman, it can be brutal. And whether you're a man or a woman, it's pretty much impossible not to make enemies. Some of those enemies can be very bad people. And they don't stay in prison forever."

Blainey sighed and shook his head, still smiling sadly.

"I know what you're getting at," he said. "It was the same five years ago. The police from Albany wanted to know about enemies she'd made there. They were just sure the killer had to be a former inmate with a personal grudge."

Dwight Slater looked at Lucy and Riley earnestly.

"The thing is, I knew Marla Blainey really well," Slater said. "She and Craig here were like family to me. And believe me, Marla wasn't your stereotypical prison guard. You know the type I mean—sadistic, mean, corrupt. The truth is, a lot of people didn't know what to make of her."

Blainey nodded in agreement and rose from the chair.

"Come on inside," he said. "I'll show you a few things."

Riley, Lucy, and Slater all followed him into neat, comfortable living room. Blainey invited them to sit and make themselves comfortable. There were plenty of family pictures on the wall— picnics, graduations, births, weddings, school pictures. It was easy to see that Craig Blainey truly had surrounded himself with the best of memories.

As Blainey opened a roll-top desk and shuffled through its contents, Riley's eyes fell upon a photograph of Marla Blainey in her correction officer's uniform. The woman was tall like her husband, with a similar strong, determined face. Even so, she had a smile that fairly lit up the living room even five years after her horrible death.

When Blainey found what he'd been looking for, he handed Riley and Lucy each a couple of handwritten letters. Just a glance at the letters was enough to surprise Riley.

They were thank-you messages from former inmates at the prison where Marla had worked. The men wrote to thank her for kindnesses she had showed them during their incarcerations—a word of encouragement, something to read, a bit of useful advice. The men had clearly put their criminal lives behind them. They felt that they owed at least a little of their success in the world outside to Marla.

Blainey talked while they read.

"I don't want to give the impression that Marla had an easy time with her job, or that everybody liked her. She was surrounded all day long by bad people—liars and manipulators, most of them. She didn't let herself get drawn into inappropriate friendships. She was a prison guard, and of course some of the prisoners had no use for her, actually hated her. Even so, I don't think she ever *made* any real enemies, even there."

While Blainey spoke, Dwight Slater looked around the room, enjoying his own share of memories. He said, "I talk to the warden from time to time, and he still says she probably did more genuine good there than the social workers on his staff. She was like that with everybody."

Riley looked at Lucy and saw that she shared her surprise. Who would have thought that a female prison guard would have been such a beloved character? And why on earth had someone chosen to take her life in such a hideous manner?

Blainey's hospitable smile widened.

"Well, I'm sure you've got more questions," he said. "Would you like something to drink? Maybe some iced tea? I brewed some fresh just a little while ago."

"That would be nice," Riley said.

"Yes, please," Lucy said.

Riley nodded in agreement, but her mind was already elsewhere. She was beginning to feel familiar nudges just beneath her conscious awareness. She knew that her ability to get inside the mind of a murderer was rare, and she also knew that she was usually right about whatever came to her.

That meant there was something else she really needed to see.

Something important.

Chapter 11

A short time later, Riley and Lucy were in their car again, following along behind Slater. As always when approaching a crime scene, Riley felt her senses quicken into sharper alertness.

It hadn't been easy to persuade Slater to lead them there. As far as he was concerned, there was nothing at all to see—especially after all these years. Even so, Riley was anxious to get a look at the site where Marla Blainey's body had been left. She knew that photographs couldn't tell her what actual places sometimes could.

A short distance out of town, the two-lane road crossed the railroad tracks and continued along the edge of the river. Slater pulled onto the shoulder of the road. Riley pulled their car in behind him.

"I think this is where it was," Slater said, getting out of his car. "It's hard to remember after all these years."

"Let me look at those photos again," Riley said.

Slater handed her the folder full of photos of the Blainey crime scene. Riley peered through the trees at the side of the road. The bank sloped sharply down to the river's edge, which was only about fifteen feet away.

Riley compared the spot to a photo of the body that had been taken from the road. The underbrush had changed over the years, and for a moment it was hard to see any resemblance between the photo and the actual place.

In the photo, she saw that Marla's body, bound in chains and a straitjacket, lay in a heap against a fallen tree trunk. Riley stepped into the long grass beside the road. There it was, the same tree trunk down there next to the water's edge.

"You're right, this is the place," she told Slater. "How do you think he got the body down there?"

Slater shrugged. "There wasn't much to it," he said. "He pulled his vehicle about where we are right now. Then he just rolled the body down the bank. The grass and brush were mashed down all the way."

He pointed to the photo Riley was holding.

"You can see just the edge of a tire track right there on the shoulder," he said. "Probably a van, but we couldn't track down the vehicle. Nobody noticed the body for several days—not until someone saw buzzards circling."

As Riley compared the photo and the actual scene, she realized that she was standing on the exact spot where the killer had dumped the body. She gazed down the slope for a long moment, taking in the scene. She began to picture the chained and straitjacketed body rolling down the hill. Then she noticed that Lucy was staring at her intently. It struck her as odd. She returned Lucy's gaze with quizzical look.

"Oh, I'm sorry for staring," Lucy said, a bit embarrassed. "It's just that … well, I've heard you've got uncanny instincts when you're at a crime scene. They say it's like you get right into a killer's head, feel what he felt, see what he saw, understand exactly what he was thinking."

Riley didn't know what to say. She often did, indeed, become deeply absorbed in crime scenes. And her capacity to identify with a killer's perspective sometimes disturbed even her. It was just her way of doing things, but Lucy was making it sound like an almost legendary skill. It made Riley feel uncomfortable and self-conscious.

In any case, she wasn't getting any vibes from where she was standing, no sense of the killer's thoughts. She didn't know whether that was because the place was too nondescript or because of the other people watching.

"Hold this for a moment," she told Lucy, handing her the folder.

Then Riley scrambled down the slope, leaving Lucy and Slater watching in surprise.

"You be careful," Slater called after her.

"Do you want me to come too?" Lucy asked.

"No, I'm okay," Riley called back. "You stay there."

The slope was steep and more treacherous than it looked from the roadside. She stumbled down against brush and branches, scraping herself a good bit along the way. The sharp descent was also a stern reminder that she was still hurting from her recent injuries. Muscles that had just started to feel better suddenly began to ache again.

Finally, she reached the bottom of the slope. She stood beside the fallen log, only about a yard away from the water's edge. This was it—the place where Marla's body had fallen and stayed until it was discovered. The quiet was interrupted by the noise of a speedboat tearing down the river a short distance away. Its wake of gentle wavelets broke against the log, then died away into stillness.

Drawing upon the memory of the photo, Riley pictured Marla's body lying at her feet. She could see it clearly. She also realized that, if not for the log, the body would probably have kept right on rolling into the river. It had only gotten caught here by accident. Working in the dark, the killer might not have even realized that the body hadn't gone all the way into the water.

Judging from the slope, Riley guessed that the water was deep right here. Weighted down with chains, the body might well have sunk without a trace. It might never have been found.

At last, she began to feel a tingle of understanding. This woman's body, like the place itself, had meant nothing to the killer by the time he dumped it here. It might be discovered or it might not be—it didn't matter to him one way or the other. The chains and the straitjacket had been solely a matter between him and his victim. They were used to torment the women, and they had some special meaning for the killer. They hadn't been for public display.

Something drastic had changed between the two killings. Now the killer wanted desperately for everyone to see the full horror of his deed. With the second victim, he was trying to communicate something that he hadn't cared about the first time.

Riley groaned under her breath. It was likely to mean that the killer was going to accelerate. Whatever was driving him was stronger now. Whatever he'd kept under control for five years was pushing harder at him to show the world his pain.

At that moment, her phone buzzed. She took it out of her pocket. She was surprised to see that it was a text from April.

Hey Mom, it said simply.

Riley felt deeply startled by the sheer incongruity. Here she was, standing exactly where a corpse had once been abandoned, receiving a text from her daughter who oftentimes wanted nothing to do with her. Should she explain that now was not a good time to exchange texts?

Hi April, she wrote back. *What's going on?*

The reply came quickly …

School ends tomorrow. I have my last exam in the morning.

Riley typed, *Are you ready?*

I dunno, April replied.

Riley sighed. Her conversation with her daughter had already become perfectly meaningless.

But then April typed:

I want to talk.

Riley's heart surged with unexpected emotion.

Me too, she typed. *Could you wait till I get back to my room?*

April's next text took her thoroughly by surprise.

Not on the phone. Right here. Come home and let's talk.

Chapter 12

Riley came to a stop on the Amtrak platform. She still had doubts about what she was doing, even though she and Lucy had talked it through more than once. They both felt sure that nothing more was going to happen here in Reedsport. The chain killer had struck in two different towns, and whenever he killed again it was likely to be somewhere else.

"I still don't know about this, Lucy," Riley said. "I don't usually leave a case in progress."

"It's okay," Lucy replied with a hint of exasperation. "I know what to do. Interview everybody I can. Go to the funeral in case he's there. Check out who sends flowers."

At that moment, the conductor called out, "All aboard!"

Riley said, "If anything important happens, I'll come right back."

"Go," Lucy said firmly.

"Thanks," Riley replied.

The little BAU jet that had brought them to Reedsport had left almost immediately after their arrival, so it wasn't a travel option this time. Lucy had offered to drive Riley to Albany to catch a flight home, but Riley had chosen the train instead. It would take her right to Quantico, with just a change in New York City. The trip would give her a chance to go over her files and consider the mind of a killer.

She climbed up into the spacious business class car and took her seat. She had two big chairs to herself, giving her room to spread out as much as she wanted to. She looked out the window as the train started to pull out of the station. Lucy was nowhere in sight. Riley knew that she was headed straight back to work.

She tilted the chair into a reclining position and started to relax. The steady, friendly rumbling and soothing vibration of the train car helped Riley begin to process information with her customary mental skill. To begin with, there was the question of just why the killer had starved both victims. Of course he must have meant to weaken them. Riley also felt pretty sure that he had probably been starved earlier in his own life and felt compelled to inflict the same suffering on others.

But now something else occurred to her. Feeding the women would have meant acknowledging their humanity. In doing that, he might run the risk of feeling sympathy for them. They were of use to him only as objects, as *symbols* of whatever had hurt or enraged

54

him in the past.

Riley breathed deeply. Yes, she beginning to feel connected with him—much more than she had at either crime site.

He's human, she thought. *He's all too human.*

He was not some cold and unfeeling sociopath. He was likely to be capable of sympathy and even kindness. Those were the very qualities that he feared most about himself, because they might well be his undoing.

Riley closed her eyes. She could feel the staggering effort it took for him to suppress his human qualities. And weak as he was, how long he could handle the strain and effort of being a murderous animal? All he knew was that he had no choice.

Something else began to make more sense to her. The shocking staging of his most recent murder, with the body hanging where everyone could see it, was not just an attempt to shock the world. It was also for his own benefit. He had a need to convince everybody—including himself—that he was far more savage than he appeared to be.

As his desperation mounted, Riley knew, his crimes were likely to become ever more outrageously vicious. He couldn't allow himself to display the slightest telltale hint of mercy or humanity. He must do his best to become a monster beyond even his own imagining.

The steady click-clacking of train wheels was having a pleasantly hypnotic effect. Riley hadn't thought she was tired, but now she realized she'd been under considerable strain for the last couple of days. She closed her eyes.

As Riley huddled in the musty crawlspace, her cage door opened and a stream of flame broke through the pitch darkness. The white light blinded her for a moment. The flame of that propane torch was the only thing she ever saw in this awful place—aside from the glimpses it gave of Peterson himself.

Now her tormentor's face took form again as he taunted her with the hissing flame, forcing her to dodge its extreme heat. She couldn't quite see what he looked like, but his presence was becoming familiar all the same.

"Welcome home," Peterson said gleefully.

"This is not my home," Riley said.

"It's the only home you deserve."

Riley wished she could grab the torch away from him and turn it against him. But his motions were too deft and swift. All she could do was duck and dodge, trying to escape being burned.

"I'm going to kill you," she said, mustering a tone of defiance. "I want you to know that."

Peterson chuckled grimly.

"Welcome home," he said again.

Riley was awakened by the conductor's shout …

"Penn Station!"

It was time to change trains.

*

As she drove into Fredericksburg that evening, Riley kept repeating in her mind: *One monster at a time.*

The dream about Peterson had left her badly shaken, troubling her during the rest of her train trip to Quantico. Even so, she'd managed to get a fair amount of work done. She'd run searches on her laptop using the train's Wi-Fi service, and pored over her own copy of the case documents and photos. She had emailed a report directly to Brent Meredith. There was no pressing need to stop at the BAU, so she had decided to drive straight to Ryan's house where April was waiting for her.

Riley reminded herself that monsters took many forms. Right now, she wanted to focus on an altogether different monster—the monstrosity that her personal life had become. Perhaps there was hope of conquering this one, of reshaping it to a more agreeable form. After much grief and rebellion, April now wanted to talk to her. It was a positive sign. Riley wasn't going to let her daughter down, not this time.

Besides, Riley was well aware that she needed to make some serious changes in her life. There wasn't much point in waiting for a break between cases. There seldom seemed to be much of a break, and there probably wouldn't be one in the foreseeable future.

First, she figured that she had to move out of her little house. Peterson's break-in proved that it was much too isolated and vulnerable. When she'd first rented it, she and Ryan had just split, and she had felt financially insecure. The place outside of Fredericksburg had been all she could afford, and it had served to get her far away from her former life.

But the divorce would be final soon, and Ryan had agreed to pay regular child support instead of the erratic contributions he was kicking in now. He'd actually become generous, which she recognized as his way of freeing himself from any other responsibilities toward their daughter.

That was fine with Riley. She would be happy to have full care of April, and she desperately wanted to be a good mother to her. She just had to figure out how to manage her own responsibilities better than she had in the recent past.

Looking out her car window, Riley saw that she was driving past rows of attractive townhouses. When her supplementary income became steady and predictable, she could seriously think about a new place to live, maybe even about buying something suitable in town. It would be good to have neighbors, and the location would be convenient for April's school. And Fredericksburg was big enough that she wouldn't have to worry about crossing paths with Ryan.

The prospect of raising April on her own brought up another issue that had been on her mind. Riley couldn't escape the fact that she spent a lot of time away from home. She needed someone to help take care of her daughter.

Gabriela was the obvious choice. She and April really liked each other, and April wouldn't object to their longtime housekeeper being around to keep tabs on her.

Might Gabriela agree to move in with them if she could have a room and bath of her own? Or at least stay over when Riley had to be away for days at a time? Riley made a mental note to talk it over with Gabriela as soon as she got the chance.

When Riley reached her destination, she drove her car up the driveway and under the carport alongside the house. When she got out of the car and walked to the front door, she rang the doorbell, as had become customary since she moved out. Gabriela answered with an anxious look on her face.

"Señora Riley!" she exclaimed. "Do you know where April is?"

Chapter 13

Shock jolted Riley's entire body.

"Isn't April here?" she asked.

"She was, but not now," Gabriela said. "*Vente!* Come in!"

Riley stepped inside and Gabriela shut the door.

"She was here when I went out to the *tienda* for groceries," Gabriela explained. "When I came back she wasn't here. I told Señor Ryan, and he said not to worry. But still I worried. She said nothing about going out. I don't understand."

Riley's agitation mounted.

"Where's Ryan?" she asked.

"Having dinner."

Gabriela led Riley to the dining room. Ryan was seated at the table, simultaneously picking at his dinner and talking on his cell phone. Another place was set, but it had not been used. Gabriela nervously began clearing the table.

"That will be fine," Ryan said to whoever was on the phone—a client, Riley guessed. "I'll be there at nine. We'll take care of everything tonight."

He ended the call and looked up at Riley with surprise.

"I hadn't expected you here today," he said. "I thought you had a case in Upstate New York. How's it going?"

"Where is April?" Riley asked.

"How should I know?" Ryan replied with an annoyed shrug. "She's in one of her moods. She gets that from you, not me. Do you think she'd tell me anything?"

Riley ignored her ex-husband's accusatory tone.

"Where have you been today?" she asked.

"Not that I have to report my comings and goings," Ryan said. "But I've actually been upstairs all day, working in my home office. I haven't left the house since this morning. I've barely been out of the office. I've been busy."

"Did April come home from school?"

Ryan finished his meal and set his napkin down.

"Yeah, and we had a fight. Don't ask me what it was all about. I couldn't make any sense out of it. I sent her to her room, told her not to come out until she was ready to apologize. I thought she'd stayed there until Gabriela came to my office and told me she was gone."

Ryan got up from the table and started to walk away.

"Look, I've got to get ready to go meet a client," he said. "It's a lot more important than this, believe me—especially since you expect me to be so generous with my support payments. Honestly, I don't understand why you and Gabriela are in such a panic. The girl took off in a huff, and she'll come back when she feels like it."

Riley stepped in front of Ryan, blocking his exit.

"She did *not* take off in a huff," Riley said. "She said she wanted to talk to me, and I texted her that I was coming back. She was expecting me. She wouldn't have left the house."

"Well, that's exactly what she did, apparently," Ryan said. "She's probably at your house right now."

Riley felt a glimmer of hope. Was it possible that April had expected to meet Riley at her own house? Might her daughter be waiting there for her?

Riley pulled out her cell phone and dialed her own landline number. She listened to her recorded answering machine message, then after the beep she said, "April, if you're there, pick up. I came back to see you."

There was no response.

Then she tried April's cell phone number. When she got April's voice mail message, she couldn't stop herself from yelling. "April, if you're there, pick up. Where are you? You've got me scared to death. Call me right now."

Riley ended the call and stood staring at the phone in her hand.

"She'll call whenever she feels like it," Ryan said. "Now if you don't mind—"

He tried to push by Riley, but she wouldn't let him pass.

"You're not going anywhere," she said.

"I've got a client, Riley."

Riley's voice was shaking with barely restrained rage and fear.

"You've got a daughter too," she said.

Riley turned around and saw that Gabriela was standing in the kitchen doorway, looking stricken and horrified.

"Gabriela, what time did you go out for groceries?" Riley asked.

"About three, I think," Gabriela said. "April's bedroom door was open and she was there. When I got back, she was not in the house and I told Señor Ryan."

Riley turned toward Ryan again. His expression was still unconcerned. She found it maddening that he couldn't see how serious the situation was.

"Did anyone come to the door this afternoon?" Riley asked.

"I don't know. Like I said, I've been in my office the whole

59

day," Ryan said.

"Ryan, *think*. Did you hear the doorbell at all today?"

Ryan paused to think for a moment.

"Once, I think. In the afternoon. Yes, I did hear a car pull up and then the doorbell. It was after I'd sent April to her room. I'm sure Gabriela answered it."

Riley turned to the housekeeper.

"Gabriela, did you answer the door for anybody today?"

"I did not hear the doorbell ring all day."

Riley was now shaking with alarm and ager. She turned back to Ryan.

"Gabriela did *not* answer the door," she said to him fiercely. "She was out getting groceries. April answered the door, and she's been gone ever since. By now, she could have been missing for four hours. Gabriela told you, and you didn't care."

Ryan was starting to get flustered now.

"Look, you're making too much of this," he said. "It was probably her boyfriend. He probably drove up and she took off with him. When she gets back, I'm going to ground her but good. You should have done it long ago."

Riley's mind flashed back to catching April and her boyfriend smoking pot in her back yard.

"Have you even met her boyfriend?" Riley snapped. "His name is Brian, and he's fourteen or fifteen. He doesn't drive. It wasn't him, and it wasn't any of her friends. She doesn't have friends with cars. Jesus, Ryan, don't you know *anything* about your daughter?"

Riley didn't wait for a reply. She pushed past Ryan and headed straight up the stairs to April's room. Ryan and Gabriela followed her. As Gabriela had said, the door had been left open. The room was its typical mess.

Again Riley took out her phone and dialed April's number. This time, her heart dropped. She could have sworn she heard a buzzing from the bed.

She rushed over to the bed and pushed aside some clothes and her heart stopped.

It was right there.

Riley picked up the buzzing phone and stared at it in horror.

April didn't have her phone.

And that could only mean one thing.

She was taken.

Chapter 14

April cringed at the sound of the man's footsteps overhead. He was pacing back and forth on the wooden deck less than a foot above her head, chuckling to himself, occasionally laughing out loud. She struggled to keep from screaming. He had told her he would shoot her if she screamed, and she was sure that he would.

She knew that the man walking on the deck was Peterson. It had to be him. Like everyone else, April had doubted her mom's conviction that Peterson was still alive. She had wanted to believe that the murderer who had once captured her mother was dead. But he was alive and now he had taken her.

She remembered with horror the little that Mom had said about this man, about how he had treated her as a captive. But April was even more terrified by what her mother *hadn't* told her. She was sure that her mother had held back the truth of her own suffering. She always did that to spare April, but now April dreaded finding out what horrors had been left unsaid.

Even after hours in captivity, April still didn't have any idea where she was. When Peterson had dragged her out of the car trunk, she'd glimpsed a small house with a large raised deck. But how long had she been in that trunk? How far away from home had they traveled?

When he'd pulled her from the trunk, he'd ripped the duct tape gag off her mouth, and she'd still been too scared to scream. Then he'd carried her over his shoulder to the house, shoved her under the deck, slapped a barrier in place, and just left her there, still bound hand and foot. She had writhed and twisted in panic but the plastic restraints held tight.

When she had been able to stop her body from shaking, she had looked around her prison. The base of the deck was enclosed with wooden lattice. He had removed one section to put her in this cage and the fastened it back in place. She thought that the lattice was made of fairly flimsy wood—but she didn't dare try to kick it out. Not now, with Peterson walking right overhead.

April squirmed around in the shallow space. She could sit up but she couldn't stand. She leaned back against the house foundation. It was dim under the deck, but it was still daylight outside. From what she could see through the square holes of the lattice, the house seemed isolated. The land all around was barren except for a few scattered trees. She could see no sign of other houses and she had no idea how far away the nearest human being might be.

The sound of his footsteps and laughter was becoming maddening.

How could I have been so stupid? she wondered. But she knew that her stupidity had started earlier than today. She had let him set her up to be easily captured. When he'd come to her father's front door, she'd recognized him right away. He'd been the driver that she and Brian had hitched a ride with a few days ago. Now she realized that he'd been targeting her all along.

The split second she'd seen the gun in his hand, she'd tried to push the front door shut. But he moved too quickly, grabbing her wrist and forcing it painfully behind her back. He kept her arm tight and the gun pressed against her back as he walked along the front sidewalk. For a moment she'd frozen in her tracks. It was from fear, not resistance. The man had been startled and he'd staggered, planting one foot in the flowerbed.

Will anyone see that footprint? April wondered. *Does anybody even know I'm missing?*

Maybe she could have seized that moment and … done what? Attacked the man? Tried to take his gun away? It was a joke to imagine she could have overpowered him.

She kept replaying the whole thing in her head. Peterson's car had been backed up under the portico at the side of her father's house. It was a newer, fancier car than the one he'd been driving when she and Brian had hitched with him. The trunk was already open when he walked April around to the back of it.

She shuddered as she remembered what he'd done next. Still holding her at gunpoint, he had forced her to gag her own mouth with duct tape and bind her own wrists with plastic restraints. The indignity had made the horror even worse.

She felt vaguely ashamed now.

I shouldn't have cooperated, she thought. *I was a coward.*

But what would have happened if she'd refused to bind and gag herself? He probably would have killed right then and there. Her father, so absorbed with his work in his office, so lost in his own little world, might not even hear the gunshot. It would be left to poor Gabriela to find her body when she got home from buying groceries.

She'd struggled in terror when he bound her ankles together in the trunk. After that she'd been completely helpless.

Now her whole body hurt from the bumpy ride in the trunk and from struggling against the restraints. She was hungry, too, and tired. She fought down the screams and sobs she could feel rising in her throat. She knew that Peterson would kill her if she did anything to attract attention. And she mustn't waste her energy. She had to stay alert, pay attention, not miss the slightest opportunity.

Suddenly something dawned on her—something almost like hope. Her mother was coming back from her job today. She might even be back in Fredericksburg already. If so, she surely she knew that April was missing.

He was laughing louder now, and the clomping of his feet sounded like he was dancing a jig. April couldn't keep quiet a moment longer.

"My mother's going to find me!" she shouted. "And when she does she'll kill you!"

The sounds overhead stopped. All was silent for a moment. Then came another quiet chuckle.

"Oh, she'll come looking for you, all right," he said. "I'm counting on it."

The sound of his footsteps changed. This time he was coming down the porch steps. She shivered deeply with fear. Then he pulled loose a piece of lattice and looked in through the opening. He climbed under the deck, leering at her, holding some kind of metal cylinder in his hand.

What was it? A fire extinguisher? What on earth would he be doing with a fire extinguisher?

Suddenly there was an eruption of hissing white flame. Now she knew what it was. It was a propane torch. Mom had mentioned the torch. But she hadn't told April just what he had done to her with it.

"Come here, pretty thing," he said over the rumble of the flame.

He crawled toward her, waving the flame in front of her. She backed more tightly against the house.

"Come right here and I'll melt those restraints right off of you," he said.

April couldn't move a muscle. She was paralyzed with fear.

"Scared of the flame?" he said. "So was your mother. Well. Just wait till you get good and hungry. Then maybe you'll be braver. We'll just have to see."

April pressed her mouth into her clenched fists to keep herself from screaming.

Peterson switched off the torch and crawled out from under the deck, closing the opening behind him. She heard him walk back up the steps and across the deck. She heard him enter the house and shut the door.

Should she scream now? No, it was too dangerous, and besides, she was sure that nobody would hear her.

She realized that it was just starting to get dark. What would it be like after the light was gone? What would he do to her then? She wondered if it was possible for her to be frightened to death.

Mom, she prayed silently. *I beg you. You're all I have in this world. Find me.*

Chapter 15

Riley stared at the buzzing phone in her hand and knew that her worst fears had come true.

"So she forgot to take the phone with her," Ryan said weakly.

"She didn't forget. She never goes anywhere without it. She's practically glued to the damn thing."

Ryan stared at her blankly. Riley could see that he was starting to grasp the awful truth of the situation. She pushed past him again and headed back downstairs. As she strode toward the front door, she glanced around the living room, looking for anything unusual or out of place. Nothing caught her eye.

She rushed outside and walked around to the portico where her own car was parked. She saw that the garage behind the house was closed. No one could see that Ryan's car was inside. No one would assume that he was at home today.

A scenario was unfolding in Riley's head. When Gabriela went out for groceries, someone watching the house might well have thought that April was in the house alone. And the truth was, April might as well been have been alone, with Ryan so isolated in his office at the back of the house and so focused on his work.

So what might have happened if April had answered the door and found herself face to face with a stranger?

What if the stranger had a gun?

Riley retraced her steps back to toward the house. As she glanced back and forth, something new caught her eye. It was a boot print in the flowerbed, just off the edge of the sidewalk. It was too big to be from Ryan's foot, much less Gabriela's, and besides, it was extremely fresh.

Someone had been thrown off balance, stumbled, and left the print in the dirt.

Riley felt the air rush out of her lungs. She couldn't breathe for a moment. Whoever was here had possessed the sheer nerve to abduct a teenager in broad daylight. She knew who that someone must be.

Ryan and Gabriela were now standing on the front steps.

"Call 911," she yelled at Ryan. "Tell them our daughter has been kidnapped."

Ryan couldn't seem to speak. His face was glazed over with mute shock.

"Do it!" Riley yelled.

Startled into alertness, Ryan nodded in agreement. He hurried back into the house, followed by Gabriela.

Riley took out her own cell phone, wondering who to call first. The BAU hotline was efficient for emergencies. Even so, Riley was wary about calling that number. By now the FBI was teeming with rumors about Riley's obsessive belief that Peterson was still alive— a belief that no one else shared. What if she couldn't get anyone to listen to her?

Instead, she called Brent Meredith's personal number. To her relief, he answered immediately.

"Riley?" he said. "Is something going on?"

"I need your help," she cried. "My daughter has been kidnapped."

"April?" Meredith replied, sounding stunned. "Are you sure?"

Riley moaned aloud. Meredith had always been her one true ally at the agency other than Bill. What would happen if he thought this was just a case of typical teen behavior?

"I'm sure," Riley said. "It's Peterson, sir. He's taken her. You've got to believe me."

A brief silence fell.

"I believe you, Agent Paige," Meredith finally said. "Where did this happen? When was she taken?"

Riley suddenly felt disoriented, confused by her sheer panic.

"It's—I'm—" she stammered. "I'm where I used to live, in Fredericksburg, my ex-husband's house. She was taken right here. Sometime this afternoon."

"Has anyone called 911?"

"Ryan did just now."

The sound of Meredith's voice was low and calming.

"Good. Stay put. Don't try to do anything just yet. I'll put together all the information we've got on Peterson. I'll get everything underway. I'll send some agents to you right away. Sit tight."

"I'll do that, sir," Riley said, stifling a sob. "Thank you."

The phone call ended, and Riley went back in the house. Ryan was standing by the fireplace, numbly staring into space. Poor Gabriela was sitting on the couch sobbing helplessly.

"*Es mi culpa, es mi culpa*," Gabriela kept saying as she wept uncontrollably.

"No it's not, Gabriela," Riley said. She sat down beside her and patted her hand. "It's not your fault. You couldn't have known."

Ryan turned his gaze bitterly on Riley.

"This is your fault," he said.

Riley had to choke back her rage. She knew what she wanted to say.

"Damn right, this is my fault. It's my fault for thinking I could trust you with April. It's my fault for thinking you gave a shit about her or anyone else."

Riley kept such thoughts to herself. Now was no time for recriminations, however justified. Too much was at state to indulge her anger. Now was the time for cool, clear-headed action.

She paced the living room, wondering what Meredith was doing right now. Putting herself in his situation, she knew that one of the first things he'd want was a photo of Peterson. It would be necessary to get lots of copies of it out there. Police would need them to go door to door asking people if they had seen the man.

But Peterson was, after all, a shadowy figure whose past was all but unknown. The only existing picture of him that Riley knew of was a mug shot taken when he'd been arrested for a minor offense years ago. He'd started a fight in a convenience store.

She'd stored that photo in her own cell phone and still kept it there. It had actually helped Riley and Bill track Peterson down and get close on his trail once before. But would it be of any use now? Riley herself had barely been able to see him during her captivity, and she felt sure that he'd changed his appearance.

At that moment, she heard police sirens approaching. She knew they would check the neighborhood to find out if anyone had seen the man at Ryan's house, or had noticed his car. Although the houses weren't close together, several others had a line of sight to Ryan's front yard. There must be somebody out there who could help—an eyewitness who had actually seen him and could identify him.

Who could that be? Riley asked herself silently.

Suddenly, the answer came to her. She pulled April's phone out of her pocket. The number was in there, Riley was sure of it. It ought to be easy to find.

If only I could stop my hands from shaking, Riley thought.

Chapter 16

Riley's hands were sweating when she knocked on the door. She hoped and prayed that she'd find out what she needed to know here.

Six minutes earlier, she'd frantically gone through the phone numbers in April's phone until she'd found the one she was looking for. It was Brian, the boy she'd caught smoking pot with April yesterday. She'd called him and told him she was coming right over. She hadn't bothered to explain why.

A tall, slender, well-kept woman answered the door. She looked like she went to a lot of trouble not to look old enough to have a teenage son.

Riley showed the woman her badge.

"I'm Agent Riley Paige," she said.

She wasn't sure what to say next. It was truly a bizarre situation—an FBI agent investigating the disappearance of her own daughter.

The woman saved Riley the trouble of explaining herself.

"Come on in," she said nervously. "I'm Carol, Brian's mother. Brian told me you were coming."

Riley followed the woman into a spacious and elegant living room where Brian was already waiting. As Riley took a seat nearby, she observed how small the skinny boy looked, stranded in a huge overstuffed armchair. He hardly looked like the same stoned but cocky kid she had found smoking pot with April that day.

He certainly did look scared. He undoubtedly thought that Riley had come here to report his pot smoking to his mother.

He ought to be scared, Riley thought. But her own fear was so searing that she had no desire to put anyone else through unnecessary trauma.

The boy's mother stood behind the chair. She also looked frightened.

"Is Brian in some kind of trouble?" she asked.

For a moment, Riley again found herself at a loss for what to say. Of course she knew that Brian had nothing to do with April's abduction. Even so, she had hitched that ride with him. And the truth was, Riley was angry about that. She sternly reminded herself to keep her feelings out of it. She took out her notepad.

"Brian," she said, looking him straight in the eye, "April has been kidnapped."

The boy's eyes widened and he grew pale. Riley understood

why. Just a second ago, the worst thing he could imagine was getting in trouble for smoking pot. Now his fear had ratcheted up to a new level.

"Who is April?" Carol asked.

"She—she's my girlfriend," the boy stammered nervously.

"Oh," Carol said, sounding mystified.

"And she's my daughter," Riley added, knowing perfectly well how weird these words sounded under the circumstances.

For a second, the woman looked almost as if she might faint. She walked unsteadily to another chair and sat down.

"I'm so sorry," she blurted out. "How terrible."

Riley, too, felt a terrible surge of emotion. It was anger and fear all mixed together. For a moment, she was afraid that she'd go to pieces right there and then. Why had she let herself get into this situation? Why hadn't she waited until another agent was available to do this—someone whose nerves weren't raw and exposed?

She wished Bill were here. Or Lucy. Lucy would be exactly the kind of presence she needed right now—calm, intelligent, and compassionate. It really ought to be Lucy asking these questions, not Riley.

But there was nothing to be done about it now. And there was no time to lose. From her own experience, Riley could imagine all too well what April was going through. But what she didn't know was how long April might have to live.

Brian and his mother were both staring at her. After a moment Carol asked shakily, "But what does Brian ... what does my son have to do with it?"

Riley swallowed hard and managed to speak in a steady voice.

"Brian, you and April hitched a ride to my house the other day. I think the man who drove you took April."

"Oh my God," the boy said with a gasp.

"I need for you to tell me everything you can about that day. What kind of car was it?"

Brian paused, trying to remember.

"It was a Ford, I think. Yeah, a Focus, kind of old, 2010 maybe."

"What color was it?"

"Gray. It was kind of beat-up. There was a big dent in the passenger door."

Riley breathed a little easier as she jotted down the information. Whatever she might think of the boy, it was clear that he wanted to help. But the most important question was coming next. She took out her cell phone and brought up Peterson's photo. She looked at it without showing it to him.

"What did the man look like?" she asked.

"He was a big guy. Not fat, but tall, and—wide, I guess."

Riley felt even more heartened. Although she hadn't gotten a very good look at Peterson during her captivity, she remembered him as being an imposing presence. The mug shot said that he was over six feet tall.

"That's good," Riley said. "Go on."

"He had kind of shaggy hair," Brian said. "And he had stubble on his chin. But it didn't look like he'd forgotten to shave. It was more like a fashion kind of thing."

Riley compared the boy's description to the photo. In it Peterson was shorthaired and cleanly shaved. She'd remembered him without stubble. She'd been right in assuming that Peterson's appearance had changed.

The boy was struggling now to remember more.

"What about the shape of his face?" Riley said.

"Oh, yeah, I remember. He had a pretty big square chin."

Riley remembered the man's jutting chin, how it protruded in the light from the propane torch. The same chin was clearly visible in the photo on her cell phone.

She thought fleetingly of showing Brian the photo to see if he recognized the man. She quickly decided against it. She no longer harbored the faintest doubt that the driver had been Peterson. But she also knew that she still had to persuade her colleagues at the BAU. For that, it would be best for Brian to describe the driver solely from memory. It mustn't look as though Riley had influenced him.

Riley turned toward the boy's mother.

"Carol, I need for you and Brian to come with me to the police station," she said.

The woman's lips were trembling and her voice was shaky.

"Do I need to call our lawyer?" she asked.

"It's nothing like that," Riley said. "Brian's not in any trouble. I just need him to give a description to a sketch artist. He's a very good observer and it will be helpful."

Carol looked relieved.

"Let's go, then," she said. "We'd be glad to help out however we can."

Riley was grateful for their willingness to help. She would get the boy started with a police artist and leave them there.

Then she would go to BAU and get what she needed to track Peterson down—and kill him.

Chapter 17

The FBI Behavioral Analysis Unit buzzed with activity as agents went about trying to locate April. Now they all knew that Riley had been right all along. Peterson was still alive, and as much of a threat as ever. The flyer had put any remaining skepticism to rest, and some of the agents looked as embarrassed as she thought they should be.

The mug shot of Peterson and the sketch that had been made from Brian's description were side by side on the flyer. Both showed an ordinary-looking man who might not stand out in a crowd except for his large size and prominent jaw. The resemblance between the sketch and the photo was unmistakable.

Riley wished she could feel vindicated. Instead, she felt utterly wretched.

Meredith stepped into her doorway, his craggy features knotted with sympathetic concern.

"How are you holding up?" he asked Riley.

Riley swallowed hard. She couldn't let herself cry. She had to hold herself together.

"I feel so guilty," she said. "Does that make sense?"

"No," Meredith replied. "But nothing does at a time like this."

Riley nodded. Meredith was absolutely right. She ought to know that as well as anybody. But after all her years as a field agent, she'd never been in this position. She'd been threatened, but she'd only observed this kind of terror from the outside. These emotions were new to her.

"Have you got any news?" Riley asked.

Meredith sighed wearily. "Not much," he said. "We've got cops going door to door in your husband's neighborhood with the flyer. Nobody recognizes Peterson so far."

"What about the car?" Riley asked.

"The Fredericksburg cops located the car the boy described. Peterson had stolen it. It was found abandoned not long after he gave the kids a ride. A neighbor across the street said that she noticed a black Cadillac backed up in your ex-husband's driveway. It was probably stolen too, and we're trying to find out about it. But the neighbor didn't see anything that happened."

Riley's heart hung on Meredith's every word, listening for some reason to hope. She didn't hear much to encourage her.

Meredith gazed at Riley for a moment. Then he said, "There's nothing you can do here right now. I don't suppose I could talk you into going home and getting some sleep."

Riley shook her head.

"It's still early," she said.

Besides, she knew she wouldn't be able to sleep until April was found. She doubted that much of the BAU would sleep until then either.

"Okay," Meredith said. "I'll let you know when we know more."

He left her office. Riley stared at the flyer again. She picked apart Meredith's choice of words just now. He'd said "*when* we know more." He hadn't said *if.* Riley tried to take comfort in that. Of course she knew that Meredith had chosen his words carefully. Did he really hold out any hope that April would be found alive?

Right then she heard a familiar voice from her doorway.

"Riley."

She turned around and saw Bill standing there.

"I heard," he said.

His eyes were full of concern. They showed no trace of anger or resentment. Whatever bad blood had been between them recently, Riley knew that it had evaporated in the face of this tragedy.

Riley made one last vain attempt to keep her emotions under control. But then it hit her that she didn't need to. Her friend was back—a friend who understood her better than anybody in the world.

Tears burst from her eyes and she leaped to her feet. She threw herself into Bill's arms.

"Oh, Bill, you're here, you're here."

She sobbed uncontrollably as Bill rocked her gently in his arms.

*

Bill was driving the SUV they'd taken out at Quantico. In the passenger seat beside him Riley was loading four three-inch shells into a Remington 870 twelve-gauge shotgun that she cradled in her lap. She'd requested the gun at the BAU before they left for D.C.

"Remember, that thing's a SWAT weapon," Bill said. "We're just likely to be interviewing civilians for a while."

"I'll leave it in the SUV for now," Riley replied.

Bill knew that he'd been right to come with her. His best friend

73

was emotionally raw and in need of his presence. Abandoning their partnership when she was in such dire straights would have been all wrong. He was aware that his taking off tonight could mark the end of his shaky marriage, but he couldn't let Riley go without him.

She was brilliant but she could be foolhardy. She had come so close to being killed when she'd struck out alone on their last case, and he couldn't let that happen again.

"Talk to me," Bill said. "About Peterson. Have you found out anything since we last hunted him down?"

"He's changing, Bill," Riley said.

"How?"

"It's hard to pin it down exactly."

After a brief silence, Bill nudged her thoughts again. "Riley, I hate to ask you to remember it all. But think back to things that he said to you when he was holding you. Does anything stick out in your mind?"

"He told me once, 'You're not my type,'" she said.

"Hmm, okay, you weren't his type," Bill mused. "Did he say anything else?"

"Yeah, he went on to say something like, 'But I like you anyway. You're opening my horizons.'"

"What do you think he meant?"

"There's so much we don't know about him," Riley said. "Nobody is sure just how many women he's tortured and killed. The only ones we know of are the four that were found in shallow graves. There are probably more out there that nobody has found."

"Right," Bill said. "And the women we found were all markedly well-off. The first was married to a psychiatrist. The second was a newspaper editor. The third was married to a real estate developer. The fourth was high up in the food chain of a big corporation. Finally, there was Marie, a Georgetown lawyer. Obviously, this started off as a class thing. He probably grew up poor. He resented it. He especially resented women who had money."

Riley nodded in agreement. "It made him feel emasculated," she said. "So he went on a spree of revenge, targeting women who represented everything he hated. They also happened to be women who weren't available to a guy of his social standing. Maybe his first victim was a wealthy woman who rejected his advances. He probably fantasized that he was some sort of one-man revolution. So his anger had a sexual component, even though rape was never part of his MO."

74

"You're getting at things we hadn't worked out before," Bill said. "Keep going."

"And he got to be very good at it," Riley continued. "Judging from the pictures we've got of him, he's probably the kind of guy who can blend in anywhere. And the last car he stole was a Cadillac. Just by taking the right clothes and props, he can probably pass himself off as rich. He might have socialized with the women, even dated or slept with some of them. What mattered was what they represented—the kind of wealth and privilege that he felt cheated out of."

Bill grunted—the sort of noise he made whenever an insight came to him.

"Riley, that's it," he said. "You're *not* his type—not a wealthy professional, not some society housewife, not the kind of trophy he'd been looking for till then. But he liked you anyway. That surprised him. He realized that the whole class thing didn't matter to him anymore. He wasn't some lone fighter for the oppressed. He was in it for the sheer sadism—the joy of inflicting pain and terror."

"You've nailed it perfectly, Bill," she said. "He's no ordinary serial. He can change. He's adaptable. That's why he's been so hard to catch."

"Let's hope that's about to change," Bill said.

Right then, they arrived at their destination—a desolate block of condemned row houses. It was dark in the ramshackle neighborhood, all the more so because some streetlights were out. All that was left of the house where Peterson had held Riley was an empty lot. The explosion had destroyed the house where Peterson had been squatting. The two empty houses on either side had been damaged so badly that they were promptly torn down.

Bill pulled the SUV to the curb and parked. He said. "Do you want to call in the D.C. police? They could cover a lot more ground, questioning people."

"No, Riley replied. "If the search becomes that obvious, he'll get spooked and disappear. Let's just go it on our own for a little while. We've got two car keys, so we can split up. You go east, and I'll go west."

"Okay," Bill said. "But you call me if anything happens—anything at all."

He watched as Riley walked onto the vacant lot where she had encountered Peterson before. He knew that she needed to confront her demons there.

Bill headed down the street, determined to find some lead,

some answer to where Peterson was holding Riley's daughter. He knew that if he found the man first, he'd probably kill the monster himself.

Chapter 18

Riley watched Bill walk away. She looked back at the SUV longingly, feeling reluctant to leave the Remington behind. But carrying a shotgun around at this time of night would draw the wrong sort of attention. The plan for now was to search, not to destroy.

At least not yet, Riley thought.

Right now, she felt the need to reach back into a dark recess of her memory—a place where she'd come to know what little she knew about Peterson.

She walked out onto the barren lot. She'd returned here just once since her captivity and escape. It had been broad daylight then. But she had felt certain then that she'd found the place she'd been looking for. Now she retraced her steps the same way. Soon her instincts told her that she was there—standing in the very spot.

She breathed the night air deeply. Yes, this was it. There was no doubt about it. Below her feet was exactly where she'd found Marie in that dark and dismal crawlspace. It was where she'd been captured in the very act of setting Marie free. It was where she'd suffered days of pain, torture, and humiliation.

A feeling of rage rose up in her. It seemed to seep up from the ground, into her toes and feet, up her ankles and legs, all through her abdomen and arms, until her chest and head felt ready to burst with it. For a moment, the house itself seemed to be a real presence all around her.

If only it really was still here, she thought. *If only* he *were here.*

How gladly she'd do what she'd done before—beat the man nearly unconscious, open his propane tanks, throw a match inside, and watch the whole place erupt into a fiery explosion.

If only it could be her own life on the line again and not April's.

When she turned back toward the street, she spotted a vagrant who looked like he must be familiar with this part of town. She stopped the man and showed him the flyer.

"Have you seen this man?" she asked.

The vagrant answered without even a moment's hesitation.

"Yep, I've seen him several times. It's the guy in these pictures, all right—a tall guy with a big chin. He comes here almost every day. Early this morning was the most recent. I was across the street there, sitting on the curb. He came walking right along here, like he always does. He stood on the sidewalk about where we are now, just looking across this lot here. And then he walked over where you were, ma'am. He always does that. He stands there looking down at the ground, just like you did. He always says something too, but I'm never close enough to hear him."

Riley could barely contain her excitement.

"Does he come here in a car?" she asked.

The vagrant scratched his head. "Not so's I know about." He pointed west. "Today he went off that way. I always keep watching as he goes, because he strikes me as odd somehow. He always turns off onto one of the side streets. Maybe he keeps a car parked nearby, or maybe not. I don't know."

"Thank you—oh, thank you," Riley sputtered. She reached into her purse for her wallet. It was hardly professional procedure to give money to helpful witnesses, but she couldn't help herself. She handed the man a twenty-dollar bill.

"Much obliged," he said. Then he went rattling away with his shopping cart.

It was all Riley could do to keep from hyperventilating. She took a long, slow breath. He really was here. Maybe he was close by right now. Maybe he even lived near here. Maybe she was getting close to finding April right now.

*

After hours of walking, walking, walking, Riley still had found out nothing. Absolutely nothing. She'd prowled every street all the way to Georgetown, talking to everyone she met. Some people had recognized the man on the flyer, and two said they'd seen him recently driving a Cadillac. But nobody she talked to could to pin down where he might be.

She hoped that Bill was doing better, wherever he was right now. She doubted it.

Peterson has got me beat, she thought in despair, turning to head back to the SUV. *I'm doing everything wrong.*

To make matters worse, a light drizzle started to fall. Within seconds, it turned into a steady rain. She'd be soaked to the skin long before she got back to the vehicle. She was relieved to see that a bar up ahead was still open. She went inside and sat down on a barstool.

While the bartender was busy helping another customer, Riley wondered what to order. Anything alcoholic was out of the question. She'd stopped drinking altogether after that drunken call to Bill that had nearly destroyed their relationship. Now was no time to start again.

Or was it?

Riley's eyes scanned the rows of bottles lined up against the mirror behind the bar. Her gaze fell upon the bourbon bottles— especially the hundred-proof brands. It was so, so easy to imagine the rough, burning, comforting feeling of gulping down a shot. It was easy, too, to imagine gulping down another, and another, and another …

And why not, after all? She'd done all she could. The situation was hopeless, at least for now. Some whiskey was just what she needed to relax her, to give her shattered nerves some welcome relief.

The beefy bartender stepped toward her.

"What'll you have, lady?" he asked.

Riley didn't answer.

"Lady, last call is in five minutes," he said.

She thought about it. In five minutes, she could put away a lot of whiskey. Still, she struggled. April was out there, in a monster's clutches. What did she think she was doing, even *thinking* about having a drink?

A tall, rough-looking man leaned on the bar next to her. He was too close to her for her liking.

"Come on, little lady," he purred. "What'll you have? It's on me."

Riley's jaw clenched. The last thing she needed right now was some jerk coming on to her.

"I don't drink," she said in a tight voice.

She felt relieved at the sound of her own words. There, it was said, and she felt good about her decision.

The man chuckled. "Don't knock it if you ain't tried it," he said.

Riley smirked a little. Who did this guy think she was? Did he really think she'd never had a drink before? Maybe in the dim light of this place he couldn't see how old she was. Or maybe he was just too damn drunk to see straight.

"Give me a club soda," Riley said to the bartender.

"Naw, we'll have none of that," the man next to her said. "I know just the drink you'd like." Looking up at the bartender, he said, "Clyde, mix this girl a strawberry daiquiri. Put it on my tab."

"Bring me a club soda," Riley insisted grimly.

The bartender shrugged at the man. "The lady says a club

soda," he said. He opened the stainless steel refrigerator, pulled out a bottle, and snapped it open.

"Have it your way, bitch," the man said.

Riley's nerves quickened.

"What did you say?" she asked.

But the man was walking away from her toward the door. He called to a friend who was sitting alone at a table.

"C'mon, Red. It's closing time."

The friend got up and the two men left the bar.

Fighting down her anger, Riley paid for the club soda. She quickly drank it straight out of the bottle. She put some change on the bar for a tip.

"Thanks," she said to the bartender. The place had emptied out and she was the last to leave. When she walked out the door, she was relieved to see that the rain had stopped for now. The night was still damp and dark, and it would probably rain again soon.

As the bar door closed behind her, she felt a strong hand grip her arm—and she heard that familiar ugly voice.

"Hello, there, little lady."

Riley turned to face the leering man. She could feel anger rising in her gut.

"Sorry about that little tiff we had back there," he said. "What do you say we kiss and make up? Then we'll just see what happens next."

Riley stepped backward, but another arm reached around her neck from behind. The man's friend had been waiting out here too.

"Don't make a fuss and you won't get hurt too much," the man behind her said.

Riley's rage erupted through her whole body. It was sheer, mindless fury—fury against killers, kidnappers, and guys like these who thought they could take whatever they wanted.

She jabbed her elbow hard into solar plexus of the man behind her, and her knee went straight to the other guy's crotch. Both men buckled over in pain. She pulled out her Glock and waved it at them. But she didn't want to shoot them. She wanted to beat them both to a bloody pulp, just like she had with Peterson when she'd escaped his clutches.

She whipped the pistol across the face of the man who'd first accosted her. Then she whirled around and smashed the heel of her hand into the other guy's face. She felt and heard the bridge of his nose breaking.

After that, everything came automatically to her, a deeply

satisfying sequence of kicks and punches, turns and slices. When she stopped, both men were lying on the sidewalk, groaning in pain.

Riley, unable to stop her flood of rage, her desire for revenge, bent over and lowered her Glock to the head of the first man. She pulled back the pin with a satisfying click.

The man looked up, eyes wide with terror, and suddenly peed his pants.

"Please," he whimpered. "Don't kill me."

He was pathetic.

Riley knew it was illegal, what she was doing, aiming a gun at an unarmed civilian; she knew it was immoral, too, despite what he had done. She was going too far.

Yet she couldn't stop herself. As she knelt there, she felt her hand trembling with rage, and for a moment felt she might really kill him. She tried to stop herself, but it was an epic battle within. There had been too many demons—and too few outlets.

Finally, Riley put her Glock back in its holster, feeling her fury draining away. Should she arrest these guys? No, it would take too much time and she had more important things to do.

"If I ever see your face again," she whispered, "I will kill you."

She stood and the men scurried to their feet and limped away, never once, in their terror, looking back.

Chapter 19

Riley was crouched in the dark again. She could smell the mold and mildew of the crawlspace, feel the dirt underneath her. But this time she was ready. She was gripping the Remington tightly. It was loaded and the safety was off.

"Show yourself, you son of a bitch," she growled.

It was so dark that she couldn't see anything, not even her weapon. But the second she saw the light of that flame, she meant to blast away at Peterson.

But then she heard the familiar low chuckle.

"You don't think I'm going to make it that easy, do you?"

She swiftly pointed the gun in the direction of the voice. But suddenly the sound came from a different direction.

"I'm hard to see without my torch, eh?"

She pointed the gun in the new direction, but now the voice came from directly behind her.

"Give it up," he said. "I'm getting better and better at this."

The voice was to her right now.

"And I'm having a great time."

Now it moved to her left.

"You'll never get to her on time."

She raised the gun and fired it.

Riley awoke to the sound of Bill's voice.

"Here's something to eat."

She opened her eyes, shuddering from her nightmare. She found herself lying down in the back of the SUV. Bill was sitting in the car door with a paper bag and two cups of steaming hot coffee.

Riley remembered now—the long futile search, asking questions that led nowhere, and the fight outside the bar. She'd come back to the SUV to lie down. She'd meant only to take a short nap.

"What time is it?" she asked.

"About four," Bill said.

Riley sat up and saw that the SUV was now in a small parking lot.

"Why did you let me sleep?"

Bill fished around for the contents of the bag.

"There was no one left to talk to—at least no one sober. Anyhow, you looked like you'd had enough activity for one night. I slept a little too. When I woke up, I drove to this little convenience

82

store I checked on last night. It's always open."

He handed her a paper cup of coffee and a wrapped sandwich.

"Thanks," Riley said, grateful that he wasn't asking her any questions. She didn't want to talk about her temptation to have a drink, nor about how she'd pulverized those two guys. She unwrapped the sandwich. It was egg and sausage and she bit into it eagerly. She was very hungry.

"I've got some good news," Bill said. "The cashier at the diner changed since I first went by there. The new guy told me that he's seen Peterson. He thinks he works in a neighborhood grocery store near here."

Riley took a final gulp of coffee.

"What are we waiting for?"

Riley went into the store to use the restroom. When she came out, she and Bill walked the few blocks to the little grocery store. It looked like a family-owned business. Lights were on inside, but Riley's heart sank to see that the store wouldn't be open until nine. Then she looked through the wired-mesh glass panel in the door and spotted movement inside. Someone was bending over a box, pulling things out.

Riley knocked hard on the door. A small, dark-skinned woman stood up and glared at her, then continued putting merchandise on a shelf. It was probably the owner, stocking shelves during the store's off-hours. Riley banged on the door again, holding her badge up to the window. The woman came to the door and peered through it at the ID.

"FBI," Riley yelled. "Open up."

The woman unlocked the door, peered at Bill and Riley for a moment, and finally let them inside.

"What can I do for you?" she asked in an Asian accent, locking the door behind them.

"I'm Special Agent Riley Paige, and this is my partner, Special Agent Bill Jeffreys. We're looking for a murder suspect."

Bill showed her the flyer.

"Have you seen this man?" he asked.

"Why it looks like ..." she began, peering at the pictures. She looked up at Riley. "I think it might be a man who worked here until a couple of weeks ago. But why are you looking for him?"

Riley said, "He's wanted for kidnapping and murder."

The woman looked shocked. "He was always perfectly pleasant around here," she said, smiling as if remembering something. "He could be quite charming."

Bill warned her, "This man is very dangerous. Don't ever let him near you again."

The woman got more serious. She pointed to the mug shot. "But this wasn't his name. It was Bruce. Let me see …"

She led Bill and Riley over to the counter and brought up some information on her computer. "Yes, it was Bruce Staunton."

The woman looked at Riley and Bill anxiously.

"And you say he is a murder suspect?"

"I'm afraid so," Riley said. "We need for you to tell us anything that might lead us to him. Do you have an address for him?"

The woman looked again at the computer screen.

"Yes, but it's out of date. He used to live near here. He said he'd just moved, and he wanted to work closer to home. That's why he quit."

Riley stifled a groan of disappointment.

"Did he leave any kind of forwarding address?" she asked.

"Or where he might be working next?" Bill asked.

"No, but he said it was in the Northeast. He said he planned to be close to the river."

Riley knew that Washington, D.C., was divided into four geographical quadrants. They were now in the Northwest, so the Northeast district the woman was talking about would be straight east from here. But it was a big area.

"What river?" Bill asked.

"The Anacostia. I've never been there but I know it's in that district."

The woman brought up a map on her computer.

"There," she said, pointing to where she thought the suspect might be. "From what he said, I'd say that's where he was probably going. Somewhere around there, in the Northeast and on the other side of the river."

Riley thanked the woman, who unlocked the door and let them outside.

"I might be wrong," the woman said. "It might not be the man in your picture."

"It was him, all right," Bill said. "Don't let him in if he returns here. Call the cops."

She shook her head and closed the door again.

Riley was already walking back to where they'd parked the car. Bill caught up with her and said, "I'm going to run that name just in case anything comes up."

When they reached the SUV, Riley got into the driver's seat while Bill spent a few moments connecting to BAU. Soon he looked up at Riley with a surprised expression.

"A man named Bruce Staunton recently changed his mailing address," Bill said.

"Where's the new one?"

After a few more seconds, Bill told her, "It's right in the area that the grocery store woman just told us about."

"Then let's go." Riley started the car.

"Not so fast," Bill said. "There's something not right here. That was awfully easy. Peterson's a smart guy. He had to know we might come around here asking about him. Still, he told his employer where he was moving, and he even changed his mailing address so we could find it? What are we supposed to make of that?"

Riley didn't reply. She just put the SUV in reverse and backed it out of the parking space. Then she turned it facing the street.

"You direct, I'll drive."

Bill was right, and she knew it. Peterson had given the woman this information for one of two reasons. He was either trying to throw her off the scent, or he was drawing her into a trap.

Riley hoped he was drawing her into a trap. She would be more than ready for him.

Chapter 20

"Turn left in fifty feet," the female GPS voice said.

As Bill switched on his turn signal, Riley felt oddly comforted by the voice. The sense that someone knew where they were going relieved her stomach-wrenching fear and dread just a little.

She'd tried figuring out the way with a map before they'd started driving. She was normally very good with maps, but her mind kept filling up with terrible images of April in captivity and Peterson taunting her with a propane torch. She couldn't think straight, couldn't figure out a feasible route. Bill had insisted on using the GPS and now the friendly voice was taking care of things.

Soon after the turn, the SUV crossed a bridge over the river. They were well into the Northwest now.

"We're getting close," Bill said.

But close to what? Riley wondered.

It was still very dark outside, and the rain was now heavy and steady. She had no idea how April was being held, but she knew that rescuing her wasn't going to be easy. She wondered yet again whether she and Bill shouldn't call in a SWAT team. They still didn't know if the address they'd gotten for so-called Bruce Staunton was correct. Besides, if it was, it was best not to have a small army storming the place. It might be the surest way to get April killed.

If she wasn't dead already.

The thought was unbearable. Riley had to put it out of her mind. It couldn't be true. She wouldn't let it be true.

"Turn right. You have reached your destination."

"Damn," Bill murmured.

Riley shared his discouragement. It wasn't a house at all, just an all-night convenience store. Its glaring interior light jarred against the rainy darkness. Bill parked the SUV. They both got out of the vehicle and opened umbrellas.

"I don't think it's a total fail," Riley said. "It's unlikely he'd give this random address if he'd never spent any time in the area. He's not here, I'm sure of it. But I also think he's been here. I think he's in the area. He likes to taunt, after all. He likes to let us know he's not afraid of us, and that he's smarter than us. Thus he would give an address that's not where he lives—but close to it."

Bill sighed.

"At least it's open," Bill said. "Let's go in and ask some

86

questions."

"You go ahead," Riley said. "I want to look around a bit."

"Okay," Bill said. He went on inside the store.

Riley stood in the parking lot, surveying the area. She saw that they had arrived in a middle-class family neighborhood, with small houses bunched close together. Across the street, the block was comprised entirely of row houses. A couple of the homes were lighted even at this hour. Riley guessed that commuters were getting ready to drive to work.

Where and how could Peterson be holding April in such a densely populated area? A neighborhood where everybody probably knew everybody else?

This isn't right, she thought.

Still, her every instinct told her that Peterson hadn't misled them—not completely. Perhaps it was only wishful thinking, but Riley was sure that Peterson had set a trap for her, and that she was getting closer and closer to finding out where it was. A part of him, after all, wanted to confront her.

Bill came out of the store, splashing through rain puddles as he trotted toward Riley.

"The guy in there thinks he recognizes the face," he said. "He thinks he's seen him around a construction site near the river."

Riley felt encouraged.

"Let's check it out."

She and Bill climbed back into the SUV.

"The guy said this street takes you there," Bill added.

As they drove, Riley's alertness sharpened. The area seemed less populated and more promising. It ought to be easy to spot an abandoned house—someplace isolated, where no one could hear a woman's desperate cries for help.

When they reached the chain link fence surrounding the construction site, Riley said, "Stop here."

Bill stopped the car, and they got out, opening their umbrellas. A large sign on the fence announced the construction of a new apartment complex. There were only a few inhabited homes nearby. The area reminded Riley of the tenement where she had been held. She felt her heartbeat quicken.

"I think we're close," she said to Bill. "Look how much more isolated this is."

Bill shook his head. "I don't know, Riley. It seems that way at night, but look at all this equipment. By day these grounds are

87

crawling with construction workers. Do you see any place where Peterson could be holed up?"

Riley looked all around. This part of the site was lighted, but she couldn't see anybody anywhere.

"There must be a night watchman around somewhere," Bill said. "Maybe he can tell us something." He pointed. "Let's go around to the other side of the site. We might find him there."

Just then, Riley heard what sounded like kids' voices. It was a startling sound at this hour, in the dark and the rain. She turned and saw a group of kids standing under an awning near the construction site.

"You go ahead," she said to Bill. "I'm going to talk to these kids."

Bill walked away, and Riley approached the group of teenagers. There were seven of them, a mixed bunch—black and white, male and female. They were trying their best to look like gangsters and thugs, dressed in the proper attire and smoking cigarettes. She also caught a whiff of pot.

Riley pulled the flyer with the pictures of Peterson out of her bag. She displayed it to the kids as she approached.

"Have any of you ever seen this man?" she asked.

One of the kids swaggered toward her. He looked like the oldest, and he seemed to fancy himself the group's leader. Riley noticed him give a silent signal to the biggest kid, who started to move around her. She knew that she needed to watch her back.

"What are you, some kind of cop lady?" the older kid asked.

Riley pulled out her badge.

"That's what I thought," the boy said with a sneer. "What makes you think we're gonna go talking to cops?"

"An innocent girl is missing," Riley said. "She's being held near here by a psychopath. She's probably being tortured. She's going to be killed soon if I don't find her."

She held the picture closer to the kid who had approached her.

"Have you seen him?" she asked.

The boy sneered again. "If I did, why would I tell you?"

"Better not do her that way, Mayshon," a younger black girl said. "She probably ain't here alone."

The boy laughed sourly.

"So what?" he said. "We ain't done nothing wrong."

Riley noticed the boy nod ever so slightly, and she knew it was a signal to the bigger kid who was now behind her.

Riley whipped around and caught the bigger kid by the wrist as he raised a knife toward her. She grabbed his arm in a lock and twisted his arm sharply as she pulled it up behind his back. She knew she could easily break it.

And yet, despite how much he may have hurt her, she didn't want to hurt him. He was big and strong, but he was still just a kid.

He dropped the knife and groaned in agony, writhing, unable to get free.

The other kids stood there, wide-eyed, staring back in panic and surprise.

"I wasn't going to do nothin'!" the big kid called out. "Don't bust my arm!"

Riley was fuming. She imagined what this boy might have done to someone else who was not as capable as she.

"I could send you to jail for that," she hissed in his ear. "For a long, long time."

The boy whimpered, while the other kids shifted uncomfortably. A few of them turned and bolted.

"I'm sorry, lady!" he whimpered. "I'll never do it again."

Riley finally sighed sharply and released her grip. She had to remind herself that this was not the enemy she was after—and that sometimes, mercy is the greatest gift she could give someone. She had to give it out while she could; she did not know if she would have any left for the man who had her daughter.

As soon as she let go the boy turned and ran, and Riley reached down and picked up the knife. She stared back at the leader, the only boy left, who looked too scared to run.

"Get out of my sight," Riley sneered.

The boy finally bolted.

When Riley saw they were long gone, she folded the blade and pocketed it. She heard a noise and was surprised to see the girl who'd spoken had stayed behind. She emerged from the shadows and stared back at Riley with an awed expression.

"That was cool," she said. "I never seen a lady do nothing like that. Don't mind them, they're just assholes. Who is this girl you're talking about?"

"She's my daughter," Riley said. "She's fourteen."

Riley could tell her words got to her. She guessed that this girl was about April's age.

"I seen him—the man in the pictures," she said. "I think he lives near here."

89

She pointed.

"Over that way, past all this building stuff, almost at the river. It's not far. It's a little house, the only one over there. Last I saw, he drove a big Cadillac."

Riley's heart quickened. She started to walk in that direction.

"Come on," she said to the girl. "Show me."

But the girl hung back.

"Uh-uh," the girl said. "This is where I get off. Last time I got too close to that place, he pulled a gun on me."

Without another word, she broke into a trot toward the bus shelter. She stopped midway and turned back toward Riley.

"He's a mean son of a bitch," she yelled.

"I know," Riley whispered to herself.

She went back toward the SUV to get a flashlight. She also wanted to get the Remington. She was pretty sure she was going to need it.

Chapter 21

He might not even have to kill me, April thought. *Maybe I'll just die anyway.*

It was pitch dark under the wooden deck. Rain was beating against the floorboards above her and dripping between the cracks. It had been raining off and on for hours, and the ground beneath her had turned to mud. Even though it was a warm August night, she was soaked to the skin, and she shivered from the wetness. And she was very hungry and thirsty.

After night had set in, Peterson had crept under the deck with her several times, holding a plate of food while he waved the lighted propane torch to warn her away from it. He'd chuckled cruelly at her hopeless attempts to grab at the food with her two bound wrists.

So now she knew that this was exactly the kind of torture Mom had endured at his hands. But Mom had gotten away from him once. Could she do that too?

At least the rain was keeping him away for now. He had been in the house for a while and she hadn't heard a sound from him. Maybe he was asleep. Maybe now would be her chance to escape.

April's hands and feet had turned numb again from being bound by the plastic restraints. As she'd done many times before, she rubbed and twisted her ankles and wrists to get some circulation going. After a moment of sharp, icy tingling, she got some feeling back again.

She rolled through the mud toward the square of lattice that he always opened and closed. She couldn't see it in the dark, but she knew exactly where it was—at a corner of the deck away from the house.

She pushed against the lattice with her feet. It was no good. It was too solid in that spot. Peterson must have unlatched and relatched hooks or bolts whenever he came and went. She couldn't hope to open them from inside, not with her hands bound.

Still unable to see anything at all, she rolled back toward the house until she bumped against the cinderblock foundation. She thought the lattice might be weaker where it butted up against the house. She fingered its edges, finding out exactly where it was nailed to a thick wooden post next to the house. Then she stretched out and pushed against the upper corner with her feet.

She gasped when she felt the lattice budge a little. It was looser here!

She pushed again. It didn't move much, but she heard the sharp, noisy sound of wood cracking. She froze with fear. Could Peterson hear her in the house? How could he *not* hear her? In her fearful and exhausted state, the noise seemed to be almost deafening to her.

What would he do if he heard and found her trying to escape? Whatever it might be, it couldn't be much worse than what he planned to do to her anyway.

She held still and listened. She heard no footsteps. Maybe he hadn't heard.

Still, she had to do all this more quietly somehow. She pressed against that corner with the heels of her wrists, slowly and carefully, hoping to push out the nails little by little. She felt a slight budge with every push. Then a single nail came completely loose.

She kept pushing and the remaining nails loosened, little by little. They made alarming squeaking sounds with every push. There was simply no way to do this silently.

Finally, with a crackling sound, the whole square section of lattice gave way and fell to the ground. She could get out now—at least if he hadn't heard that last sharp burst of noise. But where would she go, and how?

Crawling through the mud like a caterpillar, bunching her knees and hands together and stretching out again and again, she made her way outside. She managed to get across the piece of lattice without being hurt by any nails. From there, her face rubbed into the ground with every motion, scraping against muddy grass. She guessed that her face was probably bleeding by now—and her wrists and ankles as well. But there was nothing she could do about it.

When she was completely clear of the deck, she sat up and looked around. It was still raining pretty hard. A single light shining from a window reflected off the chrome trim on the big dark car, parked some fifteen feet away. In the yard closer to her there were only a few scrubby bushes. She could make out the shadowy shapes of some trees farther away, but she saw nothing beyond the trees—no streetlights, no lighted windows. There was no sign of traffic in any direction.

A sob rose up in April's throat. She was alone, and she had no idea where the nearest helpful human might be found. She clenched her teeth and forced back a wail. She thought about her mother and tried to picture what she would do, but her imagination could find no easy answers.

But her mom wouldn't give up. That was the only thing she knew for sure. Her mom never gave up on a problem. In fact, the thought whispered through her mind that her mom had never given up on *her*.

April knew that she had to make her way far enough to find somebody, anybody, to help her. Someone who could call her mother, who would arrive with a SWAT team to destroy the monster in the house and set April free. For a moment she pictured the flare of many guns firing and solving the situation once and for all.

But there was no SWAT team on hand and she had to keep moving. It didn't matter where, as long as she could get away from the house, away from Peterson.

She decided that it was easier, faster, and less painful to roll than to bunch up and stretch out again and again. She lay down and started rolling.

But just then, a bright light pierced the darkness. She froze in place and saw that the light in front of the house had come on. The door opened and Peterson stepped out. April's heart was pounding horribly.

He heard me, she thought. But the man wasn't looking around as though in search of her.

She flattened on the ground, trying to make herself invisible. But how could he not see her, out in the open like this? There were only a few shrubs that might just partly shield her from his sight.

Still, the night was very dark, and it was still raining. She barely breathed as he stepped down the front steps.

To her surprise, he walked right past her, barely three feet away. He got into the car and turned on the headlights and started the engine. For a moment, April dared to hope. If he drove away, it might give her time to escape.

But then he opened the car door again and got out. He shut the door. April choked with fear. Maybe he'd seen her after all. No, he headed straight back toward the house. Apparently he had forgotten something.

April's mind buzzed with a new escape scheme. Peterson had left the car running.

If only she could steal it and drive away! But how could she possibly do that? She was bound hand and foot.

Still, she had to try. She rolled over and over until she reached the car. Then she pulled herself to her feet and opened the driver's door. She scrambled into the seat and sat staring through the rain-streaked windshield. Suddenly this seemed like a completely insane idea. Not only was she bound, she'd never driven a car in her life. She didn't even know how to turn on the windshield wipers.

But she had no choice. Peterson would surely come back at any second. She wasn't completely ignorant about cars.

"You can do this," she said out loud.

She managed to release the hand brake, then put the car into drive. To her alarm, it moved forward right away. She hit the brake with her two bound feet and the car lurched to a jarring stop.

How am I going to do this? she wondered.

She put her bound hands on top of the steering wheel, hoping she could see well enough to avoid any obstacles. Then she took her feet off the brake and pressed down on the accelerator. The car moved forward and kept right on going.

Through the rain, she could make out the shapes of trees coming up. Steering frantically, she managed to avoid them. She had no idea where she might be going.

In a few seconds, she was past the trees and bouncing across an open field. She kept pressing the accelerator to keep the car moving.

At one rough bump, the driver's door flew open. She hadn't shut it tightly enough, but she certainly couldn't reach out and pull it shut again. She wasn't harnessed in and was in danger of being thrown from the vehicle as it lurched across the rough earth.

One bounce made her push the accelerator too hard, and the car leaped forward. For a moment, the vehicle seemed to be airborne. Then it hit the ground again and reeled ahead. In the headlights, she saw a large tree coming up, but too late to shift her feet to the brake. As the car slammed against the tree, an airbag erupted in front of her, cushioning her from the sickening crash.

April was dazed for a moment, and she tasted blood on her lips. She realized that the car engine was no longer running and steam was gushing out from under the crunched-up hood. One headlight was still shining ahead. She climbed out of the car, but she fell, rolled down a weedy slope, and splashed into shallow water. She managed to sit up and look around.

In the glare of the headlight, she saw that she was in the edge of a river. Through the rain, she could dimly make out some lights on the opposite shore. It didn't look too far away, but how deep was

94

the water?

*

Damn that girl! Peterson thought as he staggered through the rain. He clutched a flashlight in one hand and his pistol in the other.

The flashlight had caused the problem. Just a few moments ago, he had gotten in the car and was ready to drive away. It was high time, he'd thought, to abandon this vehicle somewhere and steal another one. Probably something less flashy. A rainy night like this was perfect for getting both things done without attracting attention.

And besides, he had figured, the girl was perfectly helpless, reduced to a wet puddle of shapeless fear under the deck.

But just before he'd put the car in gear, he'd remembered that he'd need a flashlight. He'd snapped the glove compartment open and saw that he hadn't left it there. It was still in the house. He'd cursed himself soundly. He liked to think of himself as better organized.

He'd hurried back to the house, still unworried—and unhurried, too, or so he'd thought. When he'd found the flashlight, he'd switched it on and realized that its batteries were shot. He'd had to scrounge through a kitchen drawer to find new batteries, and he'd barely gotten them in place when he heard the car drive away.

He'd charged out of the house just in time to see the car zigzagging off among the nearby trees and disappearing altogether into the darkness.

Now he could hardly believe what had happened. Shining the light around the back deck, he'd seen that a piece of lattice was broken off and lying in the mud. That's when he'd known that the girl was out and she had taken his car.

A lot like her mother, he thought. *Too much like her mother.*

But had the girl gotten loose from her plastic restraints? If so, did she know how to drive? She was too young for a license, he was sure, but perhaps she'd been learning. If so, she could have taken off for anywhere.

But as he followed the crazy trail of fresh, muddy tire tracks, he doubted it. Her driving had been wildly erratic, as if she'd had no real control over the vehicle. No, even if she did know how to drive, she was still bound. She couldn't have gotten far. She must have crashed the car pretty quickly. All he had to do was keep following

95

the trail. He'd catch up with her soon.

He was angry and frustrated. She'd spoiled everything. Her mother was probably tracking him right now, and might get here soon. He'd been counting on it. He had hoped to make the girl's death painful and dramatic—a fitting punishment for the woman who had thwarted him. She'd be so sick with horror and guilt, she'd beg for him to kill her too. And he'd be glad to oblige.

But now the whole thing had turned sloppy and chaotic. He simply hated that.

When he saw the damaged car up ahead, he only hoped that the girl hadn't killed herself in the crash. He fingered the trigger of his pistol, just itching to use it.

No more games, he decided. *It's time just to kill her.*

Chapter 22

Standing outside the SUV, Riley removed the Remington 870 twelve-gauge shotgun from its case and slung the weapon over her shoulder. The heft of the Remington felt good. Then she took out her Glock, checked it, and holstered it again. She picked up a flashlight and put it in her jacket pocket. The street here was well-lighted, but she might need it soon.

Although it was still raining, she tossed her folded umbrella into the vehicle. She wanted to have both hands free for whatever was about to happen next. She didn't mind getting wet.

I'm ready, she thought, clenching her teeth and slamming the SUV door shut.

She looked around, but didn't see Bill anywhere. He'd gone around to the other side of the construction site hoping to run into a night watchman. She couldn't wait for anything or anybody now, but she had to let him know what was going on.

She pulled out her cell phone and texted.

"I know where he is. West beyond construction. Hurry."

Then she wondered just how quickly Bill would be able to catch up. He might not even read her message right away if he were talking to a watchman. She added another text.

"Isolated house near river."

She walked briskly through the rain and soon passed the rest of the construction site. The road dead-ended at a broad, open field with trees scattered here and there. She knew the river must be somewhere straight ahead, but she couldn't see it.

The only light came from a small house just off one side of the road. That was it. That was Peterson's lair. From what the girl had told her minutes ago, there was no doubt about it. She approached the house cautiously, Glock now in hand.

Normally, her next move would be to bang on the door and announce that she was FBI, but nothing was normal here. Peterson was holding April somewhere. Before Riley confronted him, she needed to find her daughter and free her.

She crept nearer the front of the house and checked its foundation. From her own experience, she expected Peterson to be holding his victim in a crawlspace under the house. But this was just a low cinderblock foundation and she saw no openings in it. She thought that perhaps there might be access on another side.

Riley moved quietly around the house until she encountered a wooden deck.

She's got to be under there, Riley thought.

But then her eyes fell on a broken piece of lattice lying on the ground, leaving an opening under the deck. She bent down and used her flashlight to look inside. No one was there, although she could see where the muddy ground was gouged. Someone had been under there recently. It had to have been April.

But where was she? Had she gotten away, or had Peterson hauled her out, planning to do away with her?

Riley's pulse was pounding. No longer worrying about being heard or seen, she rushed up onto the lighted deck and to the window. She could see no one inside the house. Then she tried the door. It was locked. She smashed the window, reached inside, unlatched and opened it, and crawled through.

Her Glock ready, Riley explored the house. It didn't take long. After a quick sweep of a bedroom, a bathroom, a living room, and a kitchen, she knew that the place was empty. But with the lights on like this, it looked as though Peterson might have left hastily. Why?

She opened the back door and stepped back onto the deck. The rain was dying down. Shining her flashlight across the yard, she saw something new—deep tire tracks that zigzagged away from the house, toward the open field. Dashing toward the tracks, she saw deep boot prints on top of some of the tire marks. It looked as though someone—Peterson, probably—had followed the car on foot.

What does this mean? Riley asked herself. *What could have happened?*

But she couldn't just stand there trying to figure it out. She holstered her Glock and slung the shotgun off her shoulder, cradling it with her right arm. If she was about to confront Peterson, this was her weapon of choice. Even in the dark, if she had a clue where he was she'd be sure to hit him.

She hurried along the muddy trail of mixed tracks. They led across a field, winding wildly back and forth to miss the occasional trees.

At last, she saw a light up ahead. As she came nearer, she saw that it was the single remaining headlight of a Cadillac that had slammed against a tree. The driver's door was open, and there was no one inside.

The car headlight angled across a drop to dark water beyond. She had reached the river. Down the bank ahead of her, someone was waving a flashlight around. She turned off her own flashlight and pocketed it.

Then she heard April's sobbing voice.

"Oh, please, please!"

"Too late, smartass," snapped a familiar male voice. "Stop your whining!"

"April!" Riley shouted.

The name was out before she could think. It was a mistake. She had just announced to Peterson that she had arrived. She'd lost the element of surprise.

Riley stepped forward and almost tumbled down a sharp slope that dropped away just beyond the tree. She caught herself and saw Peterson clearly in the light from the car. He was standing ankle-deep in the river. Just a few feet from him, April was half submerged in the water, bound by her hands and feet.

Riley realized that Peterson could see her too. Carrying the shotgun, she made her way cautiously down the slope toward him. He raised a pistol and pointed it at April.

She stood there, just feet away from the man who had haunted her dreams, and her heart slammed.

"Don't even think about it," Peterson called. "One move and it's over."

Riley's heart sank. If she so much as raised her shotgun, Peterson would kill April before she could fire.

"Put the gun down," he ordered.

Riley gulped hard. She didn't have any other course of action. April's life was at stake.

She stooped and put the shotgun on the ground at the edge of the water.

Then Peterson immediately swung his pistol toward her and pulled the trigger.

Riley braced for the impact.

Nothing happened. Peterson's gun was either jammed or empty.

Riley knew she had a fraction of a second to take action.

She reached into her pocket for the knife she'd taken from the street kid. She snapped it open and lunged, splashing through the shallow water toward him.

She aimed for his solar plexus—that soft spot where stabbing would be easiest. But she slipped in the muddy river, and the blade entered high between two ribs. It stuck there.

Peterson roared with pain and backed away. The knife stayed in his chest, slipping from Riley's hands.

He suddenly hurled himself forward again, before she could regain her balance, and she slipped on the mud. She found herself falling backwards, onto her back, into the shallow water, shocked by how freezing it was.

And then a moment later, before she could reach up to stop him, she saw his big meaty hands wrapping around her throat—and felt her head being shoved underwater.

Riley felt her world go numb. No longer able to breathe, she writhed and kicked, feeling the life leaving her. How awful, she thought, to die here, in this shallow water, being strangled to death just a few feet from her daughter.

It was the thought of her daughter that brought her back. April. Riley couldn't allow herself to be killed here. Because her death would mean April's death.

Riley redoubled her efforts, thrashing like a wild fish, until finally she managed to raise one knee between his legs. It was a powerful enough blow to take out any other man.

But Peterson, to her surprise, did not budge. He loosened his grip for a moment as he bucked. But then he tightened again, squeezing twice as hard.

Riley knew then that she would die here. That was the best she'd had—and it wasn't enough to take out this monster.

Suddenly, Riley saw an image moving fast, high above; her vision was obscured from beneath the shallow, running water, and at first she wondered if it were an angel, coming to take her away.

But then she realized: it was April. She had found Riley's shotgun, and was holding it awkwardly between her bound wrists. Given her wrist-ties, all she could grab hold of was the barrel itself. Riley watched in amazement as April, feet bound, unable to walk, inched her way closer behind Peterson, her knees scraping stone. When she got close enough, she raised it high and swung it down.

There came a loud crack, audible even beneath the running water, as the stock of the shotgun smashed into Peterson's temple with a force that surprised even Riley.

And for the first time, Peterson loosened his demonic grip on her throat, stumbling backwards.

Riley immediately sat up, gasping for air in huge breaths. She wiped water from her eyes to see Peterson staggering back, clutching the side of his head, his expression one of mixed pain and fury as he dropped to one knee. April stood there, looking stunned at what she had done, and looking, in panic, at the shotgun on the riverbed. It must have slipped from her hands. And Riley watched in horror as the current caught it and it floated away.

Peterson let out the roar of a wounded animal as he charged April. He tackled her to the ground, spun her around, and grabbed the back of her hair. With both hands he shoved her down, face-first, underwater. She was unable to raise her head, and within moments, Riley knew, her daughter would be dead.

Overcoming her shock, Riley leapt to her feet, scanning the riverbed and grabbing a sharp rock as she did. She let out a primal roar herself as she lunged on top of Peterson, swinging the rock with all she had, with a mother's fury.

Riley felt the rock make a satisfying contact with his head. It hit hard enough to knock him off of April. Riley yanked her back, and April rolled over, gasping for air. She was, Riley was relieved to see, still alive.

Riley jumped into action; she could not give Peterson a chance to recover. She jumped on top of him before he could get up.

He spun over, with a fraction of the strength he had but moments ago, weak, eyes glazed, and looked up at her vacantly as she lay on top of him. She raised the rock high overhead with both hands and held it there, arms shaking. There he was, in the flesh, the demon who had plagued her all these nights.

He grinned back at her, a demonic grin.

"You won't do it," he said, blood trickling from his mouth. "If you do, we'll be bound forever."

Riley took a deep breath, and she remembered all the ways he had tortured her, had tortured all those other women, had tortured her daughter—and then she let it out and brought the stone down with everything she had. The sharpened point entering the center of his forehead, and she let it go. It was like letting go of her own personal demons, like letting go of the boulder on her back.

The river darkened with blood, and within moments Peterson lay there, eyes opened, lifeless, the only sound that of the trickling water over his face. This time, he was truly dead.

"Mom," came the voice.

Riley knelt there, atop Peterson, and she did not know how much time had passed. She turned and looked over to see April beside her. She was crying, holding out a shaking hand for her.

"Mom," she said. "He's dead."

Riley looked back down at Peterson, and could hardly believe it.

He's dead.

A moment later there came splashing in the river, and she looked up to see Bill. He slowed as he approached, slowly lowering his gun, staring down at the scene in disbelief and horror, clearly too stunned to speak.

Behind him, Riley saw the traces of orange in the sky. It was almost sunrise. It did not seem possible that the sun could rise again on this world.

And yet rise, it did.

Chapter 23

The funeral crowd was dispersing when Lucy spotted a short, slim young man who seemed markedly suspicious. He had just turned away from the gravesite and the expression on his face was not one of mourning. Head down, hands in his pockets, he seemed to actually be smiling.

That's him, Lucy thought, her nerve ends tingling. *That's got to be him.*

She stood still and watched him as he walked by her just a few feet away. That was definitely a grin on his face. This man was gloating, not grieving, Lucy was sure of it. She turned and started to follow him.

From behind, she could see his shoulders shaking a little—from laughter, not sobbing, there could be no doubt. She took longer strides to catch up with him, thinking carefully how to confront him. She thought it best to be straightforward—to identify herself as an FBI agent and demand to ask some questions. If he tried to run, he wouldn't get very far—not with the local police right here and on keen alert. She pulled out her badge and broke into a trot.

At that very moment, a middle-aged couple stepped toward the man.

"Hugh!" the older man said.

"How are you holding up?" the woman asked.

The younger man turned toward the couple, still smiling.

"I'm okay," he said. "I know it's odd, but I just keep thinking about how funny Aunt Rosemary could be. Do you remember how she used to …"

His voice trailed off as he and the couple huddled closer together and began to move away from Lucy. Then Lucy could see hear all three of them chuckling sadly at whatever story he had told.

She put her badge away. It was a false alarm. The young man had been grinning over the kind of happy memory people often shared at funerals. She was grateful that she hadn't caused a scene and embarrassed herself.

"Go to the funeral," Riley had told her. *"This one might be the type who feels remorse. He might be there."* But if the murderer had been here, she hadn't discovered him. She turned slowly in a circle, surveying the whole scene.

It was a pleasant, sunny morning. Rosemary Pickens's closest relatives were still clustered under the blue canvas tent by the graveside, accepting condolences from dozens of caring friends and relatives. Other people were wandering away in groups.

Lucy realized that she'd made a miscalculation. In such a small town, she'd expected a small, intimate funeral—and consequently, an easy time spotting someone who seemed odd and out of place. She'd been wrong. She hadn't realized how much of the population would come out for this. Reedsport was not only a place where everybody knew everybody else, but where everybody seemed to *care* about everybody else.

She walked back toward the tent, looking over the masses of flowers that covered and surrounded the coffin. Every single plant or bouquet would need to be accounted for in hopes of turning up the name of a stranger who might have murdered the woman.

Fortunately the local police would gather data on orders that were sent through the large commercial outfits. Lucy wanted to go to the local florists in person and ask about their deliveries. She was about to leave the gravesite when her attention was drawn to a young man who was standing beside the coffin—another short, slight man who appeared to be here alone. He was rather homely-looking, with a large nose and a rather heavy brow.

Could this be him? Lucy wondered. She edged toward him.

But when she got near enough, she saw that tears were streaming down the man's cheeks, and his face was knotted up in genuine grief. As he turned away from the coffin, he took a tissue out of his pocket, blew his nose, and wiped away some tears. When he looked up and saw Lucy, he managed to smile sympathetically. He waved to her weakly, then walked away. Lucy was sure that this couldn't be the one she was looking for. His grief was too unfeigned, too heartfelt.

She felt a surge of discouragement. She hadn't made any real progress since Riley left. The local townspeople had been eager to help, but none had given her any useful information. She'd followed up on details that people thought might be important—strangers in town, unknown vehicles, and the like—but they had all led nowhere.

She was sure Riley would say that eliminating suspects and possibilities was an important part of their work.

It just doesn't seem very exciting, Lucy thought.

*

Later in the morning, Lucy reached the last of town's three florist shops. At the first two, she had asked about any strangers buying flowers for the funeral, but she'd turned up no leads. The florists had known all of their customers.

When she went inside, this store looked very much like others she had visited—fairly gutted of blossoms and a little disorderly after such intense business. But in the previous places, Lucy had detected no satisfaction at the rush of sales. Those florists had known Rosemary Pickens and were grief-stricken about her loss.

An elderly woman was cleaning a now-empty refrigerated display case.

"Are you the store owner?" Lucy asked.

"Yes," the woman replied in a tired voice.

Lucy took out her badge.

"I'm Special Agent Lucy Vargas," she said. "I'm investigating Rosemary Pickens's murder. I'd like to ask you some questions."

"Of course," the woman said. "How can I help?"

"We're just trying to cover every possibility," Lucy said. "Do you remember anything odd about anybody who bought funeral flowers here? Anyone unfamiliar, for example."

The woman looked thoughtful.

"There was a young man I didn't recognize," she said. "And there was something odd. Let me think for a moment."

She rubbed her forehead with her hand.

"Such a sad day," she said. "It was so crowded this morning, and I was running out of everything. I probably wouldn't have noticed him at all, but he stood out because … yes, I remember. He had a terrible stutter. He could barely speak at all."

The woman led Lucy over to the front counter.

"By the time he got here, there was hardly anything left in the store," she said. "He found it so hard to talk, he wrote something down. Here, I'll show you."

The woman handed Lucy one of the shop's business cards. On the back was written in neat, careful handwriting …

"Please give me just a few daisies."

The woman said, "Luckily I had some daisies left. So I sold them to him."

Lucy got out her note pad to jot down information.

"Could you describe him for me?" she asked.

The woman knotted her brow again, thinking hard.

"Oh, no, not really," she said. "All I remember is that he was young and not very tall. And of course the stutter."

"Please try," Lucy said.

The woman thought some more.

"I'm sorry, but there was *such* a crush of customers today, and I just didn't pay much attention to him. And I'm no good with faces anyway. All I remember was that he simply couldn't say what he wanted to say, so I gave him a card and a pen to write with."

Lucy managed to hide her disappointment.

"I would like to take the card," she said. "It might provide some kind of evidence."

The florist handed over the card, apologizing for not being more helpful. Lucy thanked her and left the store, bagging the card as she walked away. She tucked it in her notebook and headed toward her car, which was parked a couple of blocks away.

She felt a bit encouraged now. It seemed likely that the buyer of the daisies might have been the murderer himself. The card might yield some fingerprints, and the handwriting might reveal something. And of course she now knew something else.

He stutters, she thought. *At least that's something to go on.*

She had parked her car a couple of blocks away. As she walked in that direction, she pulled out her phone. She wanted to call Riley, to give her an update and ask her advice.

When she reached the corner and turned to cross the street, she was startled to see a white van moving along slowly very close to her. Sun reflecting off the front window obscured the driver's face. Lucy stopped on the curb to let it go by.

Suddenly the van accelerated. It careened around a sharp right turn and sped away on the cross street.

Startled, Lucy held up her cell phone and snapped a picture.

What's wrong with him? she wondered. The van rounded another corner and was gone.

Lucy felt an urge to call the local police and report a reckless driver. But she told herself that the van hadn't done any damage. It might not even have been going all that fast. She'd just been startled by the sudden acceleration and turn.

When she crossed the street and reached her car, she sat down and put through the call to BAU.

"This is Special Agent Lucy Vargas," she said to the female operator. "I'm working the serial case in Reedsport, New York. Please connect me with Agent Riley Paige's office," she requested.

"Agent Paige isn't at BAU right now."

"That's okay," Lucy said. "I'll call her personal phone."

The woman's voice took on a fresh urgency.

"You mustn't do that, Agent Vargas," she said. "Agent Paige is not to be disturbed."

"What's wrong?" Lucy cried. "Has Riley been hurt?"

"I'm sorry, but that's all I'm authorized to say."

"We're working a case together. I have to know if she's all right,"

"Hold on a minute."

After a brief silence, Brent Meredith's voice came on the line.

"Agent Vargas?"

"Yes. Is Riley all right?"

"She's all right. Her daughter was kidnapped but it's all over now."

"April kidnapped? Oh my god!"

"They got her back. Agents Paige and Jeffreys are on their way here now with the girl."

Lucy was stunned. "All right," she sputtered. "Thank you for telling me."

"You'll be brought up to date later. Is there anything else?"

"I, uh…" Lucy tried to remember why she had called in the first place. "I do have something that might be evidence in this case."

"I'll connect you with the evidence lab."

"Thank you."

Lucy was distracted when she talked with the lab technician. "I have a business card with the suspect's handwriting," she said. "Possibly prints as well. I'm taking it to the local police right now. They'll dust it for prints and I'll send you anything they find."

"Anything else?" the technician asked.

"The suspect probably has a stutter," she said.

The lab technician said he'd make a note of that and they ended the call.

Lucy tucked her cell phone back into her handbag without giving another thought to the picture she had just taken.

Chapter 24

As the van driver careened around the corner and sped away, the pile of chains in the passenger seat rattled loudly.

"Be quiet!" he told the chains.

But then came a bump in the road, and the chains rattled again. There was no doubt about it, the chains were calling for his attention. They were demanding that he exert mastery over them—or else they would prove their mastery over him, holding him captive as chains had when he was a child.

"Be patient," he pleaded.

He forced himself to slow the van down. It wouldn't do to get caught for a traffic violation now. He needed to make his way out of Reedsport without being noticed.

But he knew the chains were furious. They had expected him to take the FBI agent for them. They had thought he would strike her right there in the street where she was walking. But she had turned and seen him following her in his van. There was no opportunity to strike her by surprise, and he was sure that she had a gun.

"She wasn't right," he told them.

The road was bumpy and the chains rattled at him again.

"I know she is an authority," he argued. "I saw her FBI badge when she pulled it out at the funeral. But she wasn't wearing a uniform. We do like to see a uniform."

The rattle of the chains still sounded angry.

"She was too young," he explained. "She was really nothing like the women we chose before."

He drove very carefully the rest of the way out of town.

"It would have been foolish to take another woman in this small town," he told the chains. "We'll drive north, all the way to Albany. There are lots of uniforms there. Lots of women of the right age and type. I'll find someone you like."

The chains quieted down for a while and he thought he had made a convincing argument. As he drove up toward Albany he avoided the interstate and was careful not to exceed the speed limit. He explained to the chains that he didn't want to attract attention. Even so, they rattled softly from time to time, reminding him that they were there and they were not pleased with him.

He had lost his nerve back there in Reedsport, and he must not do that again.

"I'll find another one," he promised the chains again and again. "I'll find someone soon."

Chapter 25

"I just read your report, Agent Paige," Special Agent Meredith said as Riley walked into his office. "Congratulations are in order." He shook her hand and added, "By the way, you look like hell."

Riley smiled weakly and sat down. Meredith was right on both counts. She deserved to be congratulated on taking down Peterson at long last. She also felt like hell, although she was trying not to show it. She'd spent the last couple of hours trying to pull herself together.

Bill had taken care of notifying BAU and the D.C. police about Peterson's death. He had wrapped the wet, muddy, and emotionally shaken Riley and April in blankets and driven them directly to Quantico. Riley and April had clung to each other during the whole ride, crying with desperate relief.

Riley had taken April to the BAU clinic to take care of her many scrapes and cuts, none of which were serious. They had both showered there in the building and put on clean clothes that young Agent Emily Creighton had been kind enough to round up for them. April had settled down in the break area, and Riley had spent a couple of hours writing up her final report on the Peterson case.

Agent Meredith thumbed through the written report.

"I'm impressed," Meredith said. "This was some pretty amazing work."

"Thanks, sir," Riley said. "But he had my daughter. No way was he going to get by with that." Then she added, "How soon can I get back to Upstate New York?"

Meredith chuckled. "Not so fast. You're not going anywhere."

Riley was surprised. "Why not, sir?"

"Have you looked at yourself in a mirror? You're exhausted—and with good reason. You need a rest. Besides, you're not needed up there. That case is going nowhere."

"No clues at all?" Riley asked.

Meredith shrugged. "Not enough to go on. Agent Vargas found a florist's card that might have the killer's handwriting. But aside from the florist's prints and Vargas's, there was only a partial print that we can't track down. Vargas is just spinning her wheels up there, and we'll probably bring her back soon."

Meredith leaned back in his chair.

"Besides," he said, "the locals are doing a good job, and if any new leads turn up in Reedsport they'll let us know. The killer is probably in a completely new area by now. Unfortunately, we might not know where until he strikes again."

Riley felt strangely deflated.

She began to protest. "But sir—"

"You're going on leave, Agent Paige. Consider it an order."

Meredith craned forward and looked at Riley with concern.

"You've got a daughter who needs all your attention right now," he said. "I saw her in the break room. That's where you should be."

Riley thanked Meredith again and left his office. She went straight to the break room, where she found April clutching a soft drink can and staring off into space. Riley's heart ached for her daughter.

She sat down next to April and took her hand.

"I'm so sorry," she said for what seemed like the thousandth time.

April swallowed hard and said, "He said I was a killer."

Riley squeezed April's hand tightly.

"*He* was the killer," she said firmly. "And we took him down. The both of us. You did good back there. Don't ever forget that."

A tear rolled down April's cheek.

"Just don't make me stay with Dad tonight," she said. "Don't make me stay there ever again."

Riley was startled that such a thing was on April's mind. But as she thought about it, it made sense. She had phoned Ryan when they'd gotten to Quantico. She'd told him what had happened, but not all the harrowing details. He'd sounded shocked, then relieved, then not terribly interested.

No, Ryan was not who April needed right now.

"Let's just go home," Riley said.

"No," April said with a gasp. "Not yet. Not there either."

Riley understood this reaction all too well. Their house was where Peterson had stalked both of them. Riley wasn't eager to rush back there either. She realized that it was a good time to talk about something that had been on her mind for a while.

"April, I've been thinking about moving," she said.

April looked up at her with sudden interest.

Riley continued, "I think I will be able afford to buy a townhouse in Fredericksburg. That way we wouldn't be so isolated. And you'd be closer to your school and your friends."

She could see April's whole body relax a little.

"And I've been thinking," Riley added, "that maybe Gabriela could move in with us. I haven't asked her yet."

April smiled. It seemed to Riley that she hadn't seen that smile in a long time.

"I'll ask her," April said. "She'll do it. I know she'll do it."

Riley squeezed her daughter's hand and smiled too. She felt a flood of relief that maybe she had a good solution to at least one longtime problem. And now she was on leave so she and April could have some time together. But where? They were both exhausted and they both needed a break.

Then a thought came to her.

"April," she blurted, "let's go to New York. Let's just enjoy ourselves for a few days."

April's face brightened even more.

"Really? New York City? Do you mean it?"

"Yes. Right now. Bill can drive us to the airport. There's no need to go back to the house. Let's just go."

"But what will I wear?" April cried, looking down at the jeans and shirt that Emily Creighton had loaned her.

Riley laughed with pleasure at the so-typical-teen question.

"Don't worry about clothes," she said. "We'll buy what we need right there. We'll splurge. Get a nice hotel room and catch a couple of shows."

"But can we really afford it?" April asked.

Riley shrugged. "No, but I'll charge it up to all the vacations we haven't taken. I'll hit the savings account hard. We deserve it."

April laughed aloud.

"That sounds just great, Mom!"

April's laughter was the sweetest sound that Riley could hope to hear.

*

Later that afternoon, Riley and April stepped out of a cab in front of their Manhattan hotel. April's expression was positively wonderstruck as she looked around at the bustling traffic, then up at the towering buildings. It did Riley's heart good to see that look on her daughter's face.

"Oh, Mom!" April said. "Where do we even start?"

Riley laughed. "First things first," she said. "I guess we need to do some serious clothes shopping. Do you want to check into our

111

room first?"

"Can we go shopping right now?" April begged. "These things that Emily got for me are kind of embarrassing."

"Let me think," Riley said. "It's been a while since I've been here."

The hotel was just a few blocks south of Central Park. Riley led April along Seventh Avenue toward Times Square. She remembered a couple of shops in midtown that didn't have outrageous prices.

At their first stop, April bought ankle pants and a shirt. Riley picked out a pants suit that challenged her budget, but after all, she did have to wear something decent in the city. At their next stop, Riley had to catch her breath when she saw April in the dress she'd picked out. Her daughter was clearly becoming a young woman rather than a child.

"Please, Mom," April said. "I love it."

The dress actually was very pretty and suited April perfectly. They bought it, and they both topped off the shopping spree with shoes and handbags.

Finally, they made their way back to the hotel, laden with bags and laughing happily. They checked in and took the elevator up to their twelfth-floor room.

As they hung up the clothes, Riley could see that April was looking tired. It was no wonder, after all that she'd been through.

"I think we should stay in tonight," Riley told her. "Order dinner in the room and do our touristy stuff tomorrow."

"That would be good," April said. She went into the bathroom.

Riley stared out the hotel window. Their room had a fine view of the city skyline. She started running some plans through her head. Maybe they could catch a Broadway matinee tomorrow. She would check and see what might be available.

Riley sighed. When had she stopped taking her daughter on vacations? When had she forgotten how to enjoy one herself? When April was small, she and Ryan had taken her on vacations. They'd gone to Chincoteague to see the wild ponies and to resorts in the mountains.

But in more recent years? Not so much. Several years ago, she'd taken a few days off when April had been on summer break and Ryan had been too busy to go anywhere. So she and April had rented a condo at Virginia Beach. She'd done nothing like that since.

112

She knew that April had always dreamed of coming to New York. But she wondered if this trip really would feel to April like a dream come true. Her daughter had been through so much. The excitement of being here and shopping was sure to drain away soon.

When April came out of the bathroom, she sat down on the edge of one of the beds. She had that distant, troubled look again.

"Mom," she said quietly, "I can't look in the mirror."

Riley sat down and put her arm around April.

"I know what that's like," she said.

She didn't need to ask April why she felt this way. The poor girl's face was still cut and bruised. Just looking at it was enough to bring back the horrible trauma she'd endured at Peterson's hands.

April leaned her head against Riley's shoulder.

"Tomorrow's my birthday," April said.

Riley's heart sank. She'd forgotten, of course.

"I'm sorry," she said.

"No, I don't want you to feel like that," April said. "You've just bought me lots of things. That's not why I'm telling you. The thing is, tomorrow's my birthday, and …"

April heaved a single sob.

"And suddenly I don't even care," she said. "I don't care about anything."

"I know how you feel," Riley said.

"I know you do."

They sat there in silence for a few moments. How life had changed in just the last few days! One of Riley's greatest frustrations as a parent had always been trying to get April to understand her job—why she was so obsessed with it, how important it was, and how dangerous.

Now April understood it all perfectly. And Riley wished with all her heart that she didn't.

It was Riley's turn to go to the bathroom. But she hesitated. She remembered something that Meredith had said …

"Have you looked at yourself in a mirror?"

Just like her daughter, Riley was apprehensive about looking into the mirror. She knew what she was likely to see there—the faces of countless victims and their tormentors. And in her own face, she'd see something that she really didn't want to see.

She'd see the face of a woman who had no business, no right, to hope for a normal, happy life, who was a fool to imagine that she could raise a daughter in this terrible world. There were still too

113

many monsters out there.

At the core of her being, Riley always felt it imperative to stop them, whoever they were, wherever they were. And despite all that Meredith had said, she couldn't stop thinking about the monster who was still loose in Upstate New York.

Chapter 26

The man was nodding, almost asleep, when the chains in the passenger seat began to grumble again. His van was parked in a shopping center parking lot in Albany. The chains weren't actually rattling, but he could hear them grumbling even so. And he knew what they were complaining about. It was that FBI woman yesterday—the one he hadn't taken.

"How many times do I have to tell you she wasn't right?" he snapped. "If I'd taken her, you wouldn't be happy. You'd ask why she wasn't older, wasn't wearing a uniform, hadn't done what she was supposed to do. You'd only complain."

The chains quieted a little, but didn't stop their grumbling altogether. It didn't surprise him that he and the chains were especially at odds right now. They'd been cooped up together in the van for most of twenty-four hours. Naturally, they were getting on each other's nerves.

After the incident with the woman yesterday, he'd driven straight to Albany and made this parking lot his base. Sooner or later, he knew the right victim was sure to come by. But the rest of the day came and went without that happening. After the mall closed that night, he'd moved the van to a nearby side street and slept on its floor. He'd come back here first thing this morning.

Now it was getting dark, and he was wondering whether he was going to have to spend another night here. The chains would definitely get more and more irritable. He wasn't sure how much longer he could take that.

He, too, was tired and irritable. But patience and vigilance were essential. He took a candy bar out of his glove compartment and began to eat it. It wasn't much, but it would have to suffice for nutrition and energy. He couldn't get out of the van and go buy something to eat. The chains wouldn't allow it. And of course they were right. If he left his post even for a few moments, he might miss the perfect victim.

At this hour, more people were leaving the mall than entering it. They consisted mostly of young, childless couples and families with kids. He saw no one who came close to suiting what both he and the chains needed.

Even so, the candy bar lifted his spirits. He felt better about everything. Really, he had all that he needed in life. He was especially pleased with his van. It had brought him here years ago and served him well all this time. It was big enough that he could sleep in it when he needed to and also convenient for transporting the women. He had quickly realized that the women, too, could sleep here—the beginning of their final sleep.

And he had certainly never regretted leaving his former home. It had been the scene of too many childhood horrors. He'd been perfectly happy to drive away all alone until he'd finally decided on a new hometown and settled in.

He'd been eighteen then. He'd liked his new home from the start, and the people there were kind to him. For several years he'd lived quietly and hadn't caused anybody any harm. That had changed five years ago when he took his first victim.

Nibbling the last of the candy bar, he wondered what had gone wrong. He never wanted to hurt or kill anybody. He still didn't.

Perhaps he shouldn't have stolen those straitjackets when he was released from the mental hospital. It's just that he had an irresistible feeling that someday he was going to need them. And the chains that he accumulated little by little over the years insisted that he keep them.

But what was going to happen now? If he didn't claim another woman, he knew that the chains would overpower him, bind him up, fasten his door so he couldn't get out, render him as helpless as he'd been as a child. He needed to find a third victim, and quickly.

Suddenly, the chains murmured, telling him to look sharp. Sure enough, two women were coming out of the mall—both of them wearing nurse's uniforms. One was slender and much too young. But the other was stout and middle-aged, exactly the woman he was looking for.

He watched as the two walked to a car in the next parking lane. The woman he needed was going to drive. He started the van and drove along after the car.

As he followed the car into a suburban neighborhood, he knew that something was wrong. Even if he could catch the stout woman, he still wouldn't be able to take her. The problem was simple.

I didn't choose the others. They chose me.

The first time, five years ago, that poor woman in Eubanks had provoked him when he'd picked up some change that she'd dropped in a store.

"Such a sweet boy!" she'd said.

Those words and that tone—so condescending, as if he were retarded. It stung him unbearably, reminding him of his mother and the nuns.

It was the same with the woman in Reedsport.

"What a good boy!" she'd said when he helped her with her groceries.

Both women had sealed their fates with those well-intentioned words. But this woman had said nothing to him at all. Without such an impetus, such a provocation, he was helpless to act.

And if he didn't act, he'd be at the mercy of the chains.

The car he was following stopped in front of a house. The younger woman got out, waved goodnight to the driver, and went into the house. The other woman started driving again, and he kept on following her. He still had no idea what to do next.

But now the chains were chattering to him, explaining everything. Somehow, he was going to have to provoke *her* into provoking *him.* And the chains had their own ideas about how to do that. It was going to require perfect timing, and the chains weren't at all sure that he was up to the task. He decided to prove them wrong.

Now he was following the woman on a road that wound through a park. He saw nobody anywhere. It seemed like the perfect place to act.

"Here?" he asked the chains.

The chains chattered in agreement.

Up ahead, at the edge of the park, was a traffic light. The light was green, but the chains assured him that it was just ready to change. He carefully passed the woman's car and drove directly in front of her. The light turned yellow, and he sped up a little, as if he were meant to make it through the intersection before it turned red.

Then he hit the brakes good and hard. Sure enough, the woman's car struck the rear end of the van with a sharp bump. The collision wasn't hard enough to cause much damage, but it served his purposes.

He shifted into park, put on the parking brake, and got out of the car. The woman backed her own car away from the van a few feet, then got out, looking very concerned. He walked to the back of the van and surveyed the minor damage to both cars. As the woman approached, he tried to explain to her what had happened—and to apologize.

"I—I—I—" he stuttered.

The woman's face was suddenly full of sympathy.

"Oh, you poor thing!" she said. "It was my fault, of course. I'll

117

go get my insurance information."

She got back in the car and opened her glove compartment.

He felt exactly the surge of aggression and anger he needed.

"Oh, you poor thing!" she'd said.

What did she think he was, a baby?

He opened the back of his van and took out a heavy bundle of chains. Then he stood there waiting, holding the chains behind his back with one hand. When the woman came out again, he pointed again to his back bumper, as if trying to draw her attention to some further damage.

"What is it?" she asked.

When she bent over a little for a closer look, he brought the chains crashing against the back of her head. She collapsed perfectly, falling head first into the bed of the van, completely unconscious. All he had to do was lift her legs into the van and shut the back doors.

As he drove away, the chains were silent. He understood why. They were slightly awestruck. They hadn't expected him to accomplish this so boldly and deftly. They had underestimated him. He had proven himself their master—at least for now.

*

He arrived at his house about an hour later. He pulled the van beside the house and backed it around to the basement door. Then he got out, walked to the back of the van, and opened the doors.

There she was, lying completely still, a pool of blood around her head. He bent over to make sure she was still breathing. Fortunately, she was. The chains wanted her to be alive, at least for now.

He'd stopped along the road outside of Albany put her into the straitjacket. Sooner or later, she'd regain consciousness, and the chains had thought it best to put her in the straitjacket right away.

Now came the difficult task of getting her into the basement. The woman was slightly heavier than the others had been, and he was none too strong. He tugged and pulled until she fell out of the van, then tugged and pulled some more until he got her to the basement door. He opened the door and pushed her on inside.

As he rolled her across the concrete floor, she emitted a loud groan, then fell silent again. He had the cot ready. Clumsily, he pulled the woman's upper body up on it, then wrestled her legs onto it as well.

From that point on, things were much easier. He began to wrap the chains around and around her, binding her tightly to the cot. The chains laughed with delight. They were well-pleased with his work.

When he finished wrapping, he heard her speak.

"Where am I?" she said, just starting to regain consciousness. "Oh, God, where am I? What's going on?"

He shushed her loudly. If he could only talk, he'd explain to her that she mustn't say a word. In this place, only the chains were allowed to speak.

But his shushing didn't do any good.

"Where am I?" she said in a slurred voice, her terror rising. "Somebody help me."

He stuffed a rag into the woman's mouth, then gagged her by wrapping a chain all the way around her head. She continued to writhe and groan. Her wide-eyed gaze was fixed across the room. He followed the gaze and saw that she was staring at the little altar he had made.

A bulletin board rested atop a table pushed against the wall. On the table he had respectfully placed shoes, a prison guard's badge, a nurse's uniform and nametag, a few buttons, and other items belonging to the other two women. On the bulletin board were pinned obituaries, funeral handouts, and pictures he had taken of the flowers he had left at the gravesites.

He was glad she was looking there. It ought to give her some comfort. Surely she understood that she, too, would be memorialized there when the time came. A tear came to his eye and he thought about how he had mourned those two women—and how he would mourn this one.

But the woman groaned sharply against the gag. She didn't understand. It was infuriating. This whole thing was going to play out the same way it had before. He'd loosen the chains and remove the rag to give her a drink of water, and she'd scream uncontrollably.

Maybe he could make this one understand. He took his straight-edged razor out of his pocket, opened it, and held it close to the woman's throat, shushing again. Surely she'd understand that he didn't want to slit her throat, and that the choice was hers. All she had to do was keep quiet.

Her groaning quieted a little. Even so, he still saw a trace of defiance in her eyes. It was no good. Sooner or later, this one, too, was going to scream, and he'd have no choice but to kill her.

And like last time, he would hang her up for all to see. The warning was absolutely necessary. The world had to know. The world had to understand. The world must be told to leave him alone. He didn't yet know how and where he would display her. The chains would tell him what to do.

This was how it always went. Killing the women was never his intention. But sooner or later the chains would give him no other choice. It was just a fact of life, and he'd never be able to change it.

Chapter 27

The message came on their third day in New York, while Riley and April were sitting in the food court of the Museum Natural of History. They were eating hot dogs loaded with a variety of toppings. Riley was startled to see that her buzzing cell phone showed a text from Lucy.

"Sorry to bother U on vacation. Call if U can."

Riley's interest was piqued.

"What is it, Mom?" April asked Riley.

"It's Lucy—I mean Agent Vargas. You met her the night we had the break-in."

April looked intrigued. Riley hadn't seen that look of honest interest on April's face since they'd arrived in the city.

They'd been doing all the obligatory tourist things—visiting the Statue of Liberty, going to the top of the Empire State Building, and taking in a Broadway matinee. Still shaken from her ordeal, April's earlier enthusiasm had faded.

Riley couldn't blame her. The truth was, she was thinking that this trip might have been a bad idea from the beginning.

"What does she want?" April asked.

"She wants me to call," Riley said. "It can wait."

"Why wait?" April asked with a shrug.

It was a good question. It wasn't as if Lucy was likely to spoil anything. Riley punched the number.

"Riley!" Lucy almost shouted when she answered. "Am I glad to talk to you!"

"What's going on?"

"We've got another victim," Lucy said.

Riley's nerves quickened. She'd had a hunch that the killer was going to strike again sooner rather than later. Sometimes she didn't like being right.

"I'm in Albany," Lucy explained. "A woman here disappeared from her car. She was a nurse. In uniform, like the last one."

Riley's interest grew. That confirmed a definite pattern—a prison guard and now two nurses, all women in uniform.

"Are you sure it's our guy?" Riley asked.

"Yeah, our field office agents are sure too. The police found a small length of chain on the pavement. They knew about the chain killer, so they made a report to the FBI field office and the agents contacted me in Reedsport. Of course, the chain could just be a coincidence, but … "

"But chains sure point to our psychopath," Riley said, taking a long deep breath. Then she noticed that April was watching her and listening apprehensively.

"Why did you want to talk to me?" Riley asked.

A silence fell. Riley sensed that Lucy was getting ready to ask for a favor.

"Riley, I called it in to Quantico," the junior agent said. "Agent Meredith said they'd send somebody up to partner with me. I don't know who yet. And of course I'm already working with the field office here, but …"

Lucy's voice trailed off.

"Naw, it's crazy," she said. "You're on vacation. I shouldn't have bothered you. I'll let you go."

"Tell me," Riley said.

There was another pause.

"Look, whoever they send up, I'm probably going to be lead investigator, because I'm on this case already. I'm not sure I'm ready for that. I'm already feeling out of my depth. I was wondering if you could come up and …"

Lucy stopped again, but she didn't need to finish her sentence. Riley understood perfectly that Lucy wanted her to take charge again.

"I don't know about this, Lucy," Riley said. "Meredith has got me under pretty strict orders to stay on leave."

"I understand," Lucy said. "I knew it was crazy. Sorry to bother you."

"No, wait, don't hang up," Riley said.

Another silence fell. Riley wavered as to what to say.

"Let me get back to you," she finally said.

"Okay," Lucy replied.

They ended the call.

"What was that about?" April asked.

"There's been another abduction in Upstate New York," Riley said. "Lucy wants me to come up and work on it."

April's eyes widened.

"So what are you going to do?" she asked.

"I'm thinking maybe I should go," Riley said. "I'd have to get the next train to Albany."

April looked alarmed.

"Oh, no, Mom," she said. "Don't even think of it. You're not

122

sending me back to stay with Dad. I'm just not going there."

Riley sighed. April had a point. But what were the alternatives?

Then April said, "Why don't I come with you?"

She was smiling. Riley found it nice to see her smile again.

"Maybe I could help," April added.

"Absolutely not," Riley said. "If you come, you're staying put in our hotel room. And I don't want to hear any complaints about it."

April pouted just a little.

"Okay," she said. "But the hotel had better have a pool. And I'll have to buy a bathing suit. I'm still on vacation, even if you're not." April fell silent for a moment, then added, "I promise to let you do your job. I'll stay out of the way."

"It's a deal," Riley said. She dialed up Lucy to tell her that she was on her way.

*

About four hours later, Riley was in Albany, riding in a car with Lucy driving. They had just left April in a nice room that Lucy had reserved. It connected directly to another room where Lucy was staying. Riley and April had been able to buy a bathing suit right there in the hotel, and she had left her daughter happily splashing in the pool. It felt good to know that April was in a safe place.

Lucy drove them into a park and stopped near a taped-off lane where an empty car still sat on the road. A couple of Albany police officers were nearby. That portion of the surrounding park was also cordoned off from the public with crime scene tape.

"Here we are," Lucy said. "I asked them to leave everything in place until you got here."

They got out and went to inspect the scene. Riley could see that the front end of the abandoned car was dented, but not severely. It obviously had not been a high-speed crash. The driver's door was still open.

"Her name is Carla Liston," Lucy said. "She was on her way home after finishing her shift at the hospital and doing some shopping with a friend. That was Myra Cortese, another nurse. Liston had dropped Cortese off before she got to this point."

Lucy pointed to the pavement in front of the car.

"Here's just the trace of a skid mark," she said. "And some glass shards on the road, but that's from her headlight."

123

Riley bent over and inspected the dent in the front of the car. "Have these white marks analyzed," she said. "They're sure to be from the killer's vehicle and they'll identify the make. That also means that it has a dented back bumper."

Lucy said, "The abductor's vehicle must have stopped suddenly at the light. My guess is that he deliberately tricked her into rear-ending him. He attacked her when she got out of her car to inspect the damage."

Riley nodded in agreement.

"And we're pretty sure he's small and non-threatening," Riley added. "So she wasn't scared of him when she saw him. Have you got anything new in the way of a profile?"

"Yeah," Lucy said. "I think he stutters. I got that from a florist who remembered a stranger who couldn't tell her what he wanted to buy for the funeral."

"Good work," Riley said. "That could be an important lead."

She looked more closely at the front of the woman's car.

"The damage is higher up than you'd expect from a regular-sized car. That means probably a van or truck. We'd already guessed that he probably uses a van. What about the chain you said the cops found?"

Lucy took a color photograph out of a folder and handed it to Riley. The picture had been taken while the chain was still laying the pavement. It was a short, small brass chain, the kind that might be used to latch a door.

"It's not the kind of chain he used to bind up the victims," Lucy said. "Do you think he left it as some kind of a message?"

"I don't think so," Riley said. "He makes his statement when he hangs up the victim. My guess is that this just fell out of the back of his van without his noticing it. He probably drives around with all kinds of chains in the van."

"But why?" Lucy asked. "I mean, aside from to attack his victims?"

Riley didn't reply. It was a good question, and an important one. Whatever was driving this killer wasn't coming clear to her. She wanted another opinion.

"I'm going to make a phone call," Riley said.

She walked over to a park bench and sat down, then dialed Mike Nevins's number on her cell phone. Her forensic psychiatrist friend had a wide range of experience with various kinds of murderers and other criminals. The FBI often called him in as consultant on difficult cases.

When she got him on the line, Riley said, "Mike, I need your input. I'm up in Albany working on the chain killer case. He's abducted another woman."

"I thought you were on leave," Mike said.

Riley sighed. She really didn't want to get into this with Mike. He wouldn't approve of her defying Meredith's orders.

"Well, I was, but now I'm not. Don't ask a lot of questions about it, okay? I take it you're familiar with the case."

"Yes, I've been keeping up. He's committed two murders. Both times the victims were found in straitjackets and wrapped with chains."

"That's right," Riley said. "And they're wrapped with far more chains than needed to hold anybody. He even wraps them across the victim's mouth. It looks like he's just obsessed with chains of all kinds. He must collect them wherever he goes. God knows how many he's got at home. It's like chains are some kind of fetish."

Riley got up and began to pace.

"The thing is, I don't get it," she said. "Why chains? Why not something else? And why are they even needed on top of a straitjacket? That why I need your take on it."

A long silence fell.

Finally, Mike said, "I can think of possible reasons, but at this point it would all just be speculation. I do know somebody you should talk to—but you'll have to visit him in Sing Sing."

Chapter 28

A guard escorted Riley into a small room with cream-colored walls and a barred window. On one wall was a framed mirror that was obviously an observation window for anyone watching from the other side. The guard looked at Riley inquiringly and she said, "It's okay." He left and closed the door behind him.

The prisoner, clad in a dark green jumpsuit, was already sitting at the table waiting. He was smiling at her.

Riley wasn't yet sure what to make of that smile. It was, after all, the smile of a cold-blooded killer who was serving a life sentence. She sat down in the vacant chair on the other side of the table, facing him.

Shane Hatcher was a sturdily built African-American. Mike Nevins had told Riley that he was fifty-five years old, but he looked younger. Riley guessed that he took good care of himself and made use of Sing Sing's exercise equipment.

"So you must be Agent Riley Paige," Hatcher said. "Mike Nevins has told me things about you."

"Good things, I hope," Riley said.

Hatcher didn't reply, and his smile got just a bit more inscrutable.

He was wearing small reading glasses that were perched low on the bridge of his nose. They didn't make him look bookish, though. His face was too imposing for that.

Yesterday, Mike had told Riley she should talk to Hatcher, and she had promptly set up the visit for this morning. She'd made the two two-hour drive from Albany to Sing Sing Correctional Facility alone, because Lucy was waiting at the FBI field office in Albany for her new partner to arrive.

"I like ol' Mike," Hatcher said. "He contacted me after he read one of my articles. I've published in a few magazines, you know. I've done a lot of studying here on the inside. Criminology, mostly. I've gotten to be kind of an expert. Earned some respect in the field. I figure maybe if I can share some insights with the world, it's some kind of atonement."

He leaned toward her and added with a note of confidentiality, "I've changed a lot. I'm not like the kid that came in here." After a brief silence, he added, "But then nobody stays the same for long in here."

Riley sensed that this was true, but she wasn't sure in what

126

way. This man had been in Sing Sing for a long time. Was he rehabilitated, ready to return to free society? No parole board had thought so in several long decades. No, there was a reason Shane Hatcher was still behind bars. There was also a reason why he had survived. He might be a better human being than the kid who came in here, but he was also more cunning—perhaps more devious. That could actually be more dangerous.

He looked at Riley closely, apparently sizing her up.

"So why should I talk to you?" he asked. "I mean, what am I going to get out of the deal?"

It wasn't an entirely unexpected question. Before coming here, Riley had wondered whether she should bring a little contraband—a pack of cigarettes or a small bottle of whiskey. Prisoners always wanted something from visitors. Hatcher was going to be no exception.

"What do you have in mind?" Riley asked cautiously.

Hatcher drummed his fingers on the table.

"Well, I'll tell you what you want to know—as long as *you* tell me something in return when we're done. Something that you don't want people to know. Something you wouldn't want anybody else to know."

Riley tried to conceal her unease. This could be tricky. He very likely was hoping that she'd tell him something that he could use as leverage or even blackmail.

But what really surprised her was that he wasn't asking for this favor up front, before he'd even talked to her. Riley could renege, of course.

Or could she? Did he have her correctly pegged as someone whose word could be trusted?

"It's a deal," she said.

"Then let's get started," Hatcher said.

Riley decided to get right to the point.

"Mike tells me that you know a lot about chains," she said.

Hatcher's smile turned a bit darker.

"Yeah, I was called 'Shane the Chain' when I was gangbanger back in the day. I did a lot of fighting with chains, sort of as a trademark. That made me one scary bro, so I rose up in the ranks real fast. And I killed a few people with those chains. Never mind how many. I was a street warrior, after all."

His face took on a faraway look as he slipped into memory.

"There was a beat cop who especially had it in for me," he said.

"Swore he'd take me down, and I swore that I'd kill him if he tried. Well, that day came, and I pulverized him with a set of tire chains. There wasn't much left of him by the time I was through. It was a closed casket funeral."

His eyes narrowed.

"Oh, I should mention that I dumped his body on his front porch for his wife and kids to find. That's when I got caught. And that's how I got here. Why I'm still here."

Riley was startled by how calmly he said this, as if he were talking about somebody else. She studied his expression for some trace of regret, but she couldn't detect very much of that. His story made it clear why he had not been paroled.

Hatcher continued, "Mike told me about the serial you're after. How he binds up women with chains, tortures them, leaves their bodies all chained up. In straitjackets, too."

"Right," Riley said. "He's obsessed with chains. He seems to collect them, all kinds of them."

"I can see why," Hatcher said. "Chains give you a feeling of power. For me, they started out as a gimmick, a way to intimidate. I never expected to kill anybody. But they got to be an addiction. I really got to love them. And the killing, well, it felt just great, and I never wanted to stop. Those chains pushed me right over the edge, from a screwed-up kid into a bloodthirsty monster."

Hatcher scratched his chin thoughtfully.

"What kind of physical evidence have you got?" he asked. "I mean, aside from his interest in chains and straitjackets?"

Riley thought for a moment.

"My partner found a business card that might have a sample of his handwriting," she said. She pulled an enlarged image of the card out of her folder and passed it across the table. Hatcher picked it up and looked at it, pushing the reading glasses up the bridge of his nose.

"I take it that it's been checked for fingerprints," he said.

"Yeah, we only got a partial and couldn't match it."

Hatcher adjusted his glasses for a better look.

"What have the BAU handwriting experts said about it?" he asked.

"We haven't heard back from them yet."

Hatcher seemed to be more and more fascinated by the card.

He said slowly and tentatively, "There's something about that handwriting. I'm not sure just what …"

128

Then he snapped his fingers.

"Yeah, I know what it is. It looks just like David Berkowitz's handwriting. You've heard of the 'Son of Sam,' haven't you?"

"I sure have," Riley said.

She'd studied about David Berkowitz at the academy. He was a psychotic serial killer who murdered six people and injured seven others during the mid-1970s. Before he was caught, he'd left behind letters signed "Son of Sam." The name had stuck ever since.

Riley also knew that Berkowitz had done some time at Sing Sing. She wondered if Hatcher had gotten to know him. It would have been a fascinating relationship.

Hatcher pointed to details in the writing.

"It's the same vertical letters," he said. "It also looks tense and tight, like Berkowitz's. I'll bet your guy has a lot in common with him."

"For example?" Riley asked.

Hatcher leaned back in his chair.

"Well, Berkowitz was given up for adoption as a baby. He grew up feeling abandoned. Had a real 'mommy problem.'"

Hatcher thought some more.

"It starts to make sense," he said. "Berkowitz wasn't into chains, but I've known a few others who are. I've talked to them about it. One thing most of the chain fanciers have got in common is childhood trauma, maybe abandonment. They were mistreated with chains as kids, beaten with them, restrained with them. They were powerless, so they look to chains for power."

Hatcher was growing more animated. He obviously enjoyed having someone to talk to, especially someone he could educate.

He continued, "Of course the chains won't ever *give* them that sense of power, because chains were what made them feel helpless in the first place. But I'm sure you've heard Einstein's definition of insanity."

Riley nodded. "He called it doing something over and over again and expecting a different result."

"Now, that's not *my* profile, because I'm no psychopath," Hatcher said. "But if you're talking about a true serial killer, well …"

Hatcher looked Riley straight in the eye.

He said, "I think you'd better check out orphanages and the like. Look for somebody who's been both abandoned and restrained. Someone who's been tortured."

He rapped his knuckles against the table.

"Is there anything else I can help you with?" he asked.

Riley felt more than satisfied.

"No, that should do it," she said.

"So what is it you don't want people to know about you?" he asked.

Riley said nothing for a moment. She wavered. Now was the time when she could simply get up from the table and walk away, breaking her part of the bargain. The man posed no threat to her, after all. He was never getting out of this place.

But his eyes were still locked on hers. His will was extremely strong. And he understood her in a most discomforting way. He knew that she wouldn't break her word. Even if she didn't know why, she couldn't do that.

But what could she tell him that wouldn't give him more power over her than he already had?

"I'm a lousy mother," she said.

Hatcher shook his head and chuckled sourly.

"You're going to have to do better than that," he said. "I'm not looking to hear something that everybody who knows you knows already. Even I had that figured out."

Riley felt a chill. He probably really had figured out that much about her. She thought in silence for another moment.

Finally she said, "You told me that it felt great to kill with chains. I know that feeling."

"Is that so?" he asked, sounding intrigued.

"The other day I killed a man with a sharpened rock," she said. "I smashed his head in, again and again. And the thing is, I didn't regret it, one bit. In fact, I wish I could do it again."

He smiled broadly, apparently enjoying her answer.

"And now, if you don't mind, I'd like to go," she said.

As soon as the words were out of her mouth, she asked herself, *Why am I asking his permission?*

He really did have tremendous force of will.

"Just one more thing," Hatcher said. "I'd like an honest answer to a simple question. Do you think a man like me is worth keeping alive?"

Riley felt a smile form on her own face.

"No," she said.

Hatcher chuckled darkly and rose from his chair.

"Come back and see me any time," he said. Then with a shrug

130

and a wink, he added, "I'll be here."

*

After her talk with Hatcher, Riley returned to the FBI vehicle for her drive back to Albany. Before she started the car, she called Lucy at the field office there. She told her what Hatcher had said and asked Lucy to get the BAU team looking into orphanages, foster homes, and adoption services and cross-reference for speech impediments, especially a stutter.

"You mean checking for places that have been charged with using excessive restraint?" Lucy asked.

"Yes, but they should look at it the other way too, for records on kids who have been restrained. Especially with chains. They should cross-reference all of that with what we've projected as the probable age and build of the chain killer. We still don't know exactly what we're looking for, but it will be a start."

"Okay, anything else?"

"They should actually cross-reference for anything to do with chains."

Lucy agreed and hung up. Riley hoped that the BAU search would be more helpful than the interviews they'd done with the kidnap victim's family and co-workers. The woman's family was emotionally devastated and in serious denial. They refused to believe that she had been kidnapped. Maybe she'd been hurt in the accident, they insisted, and was wandering around in a state of confusion. Still, they were anxious for the police and the FBI to take care of everything. To find her and return her home.

The nurse who had been dropped off by the victim had tried hard to be helpful. She had described everything they'd done at the mall after work, but she'd often stopped and corrected her story, putting events in a different order.

"I'm so sorry," she had wailed. "I know I should remember more. We were just having a good time shopping after work. Everything was so normal."

Riley had asked the distraught woman to call if she thought of anything else, even a small detail. But that prospect didn't seem likely.

Riley was feeling grim as she drove back to Albany. But she hoped that the BAU would bring up something useful by the time she arrived.

131

*

Less than two hours later, Riley walked into the front office of the FBI field office. When she saw who was there with Lucy, she stopped dead in her tracks. The man signing in was Bill Jeffreys. He turned away from the desk just in time to see Riley.

"What are you doing here?" he asked.

"What are *you* doing here?" Riley replied.

"Meredith sent me to help Agent Vargas," he said. "I know he didn't send you. You're supposed to be on leave. He told me it was an order."

Lucy looked mortified.

"Oh, no," she said. "This is all my fault."

"No, it's not, Lucy," Riley said wearily. "It was my decision."

Bill looked as though he could hardly believe his eyes.

"Riley, what do you think you're doing? You got fired once. Do you want to get fired again? And after everything you went through with your daughter, do you think you're in any state of mind to go back to work?"

"There's nothing wrong with my state of mind," Riley said.

Bill shook his head. "And what about April?" he asked. "Where is she right now?"

"She's right here in Albany," Riley said. "She's safe, Bill, and she's going to stay that way."

Lucy tried to step between Riley and Bill. She said, "Agent Jeffreys, I take full responsibility. I asked her to come."

Before Bill could reply, there came a tentative voice from nearby.

"Um, Agent Paige …"

Riley and her companions turned around. A shy, nerdish young technician had just come into the area.

"I think we've got some leads," he said.

132

Chapter 29

Things weren't at all comfortable in the field office meeting room. Bill was clearly not pleased by Riley's presence in Albany. He and Lucy sat at one side of the table, going over the list of possible suspects. Seated directly across from them, Riley made sure that she got a look at every item under scrutiny.

Paul Nooney, the rather mousy technician who had called them in from the front office, sat nearby, sorting through his folder of possible suspects. His laptop was open, and he was intermittently running searches.

"What about this one?" Bill asked, passing Lucy a sheet of paper.

"I don't think so," Lucy said. "This guy resisted arrest, and it took three cops to subdue him. We're not looking for somebody that strong."

Riley reached out and slid the paper where she could see it. She just nodded.

"Hey, here's somebody," Nooney said. "His name is Wayne Turner, and he lives up in Walcott. He's twenty-eight years old, five foot six, weighs a hundred and fifteen pounds. According to his sheet, he's got a slight stutter. He was an orphan and spent some time in an orphanage before he was adopted. Seven months ago, he was arrested for attacking a woman outside a movie theater. That's his only offense, but still …"

Riley's interest was piqued.

"Can you find anything else about him?" she asked.

Nooney ran a search on his laptop. "He recently got a job with a hardware wholesale company," he said. Looking up at the others, he added, "That means he'll have access to lots of chains. It also means he'll be traveling up and down the river valley a lot. Maybe he already is."

Bill looked at Lucy and said, "Sounds like someone we should pay a visit to."

Lucy nodded, and she and Bill stood up. Riley stood up too.

"Not you," Bill said to Riley. "You're not assigned to this case. Just go back to your hotel and spend some time with April. She needs your attention."

Riley felt stymied. She heard the implied "and we don't" at the end of his sentence. She knew that Bill had a point. April had been doing just fine but she would probably appreciate some company.

Then Lucy said, "I'll go back to the hotel. I can do some work there and also check in on April."

Riley and Bill both looked at Lucy with surprise.

Lucy shrugged and said, "Look, I don't understand all that's going on between you two, but you've got to sort it out. And I'll only get in the way. Go. Do your job."

Bill leveled his gaze at Riley. Then he growled, "Okay, let's go."

*

During the half-hour drive from Albany to Walcott, Riley tried to make conversation with Bill a few times. It didn't go very well. She ventured once or twice to apologize for coming to Albany against Meredith's orders. She'd also suggested that maybe they needed to discuss some sources of the tension between them, including her drunken phone call.

But Bill really didn't want to talk about any of it. That worried Riley. His taciturn attitude didn't bode well for interviewing a potential suspect.

Bill parked the FBI car in front of a small, white house—an ordinary-looking little home in an ordinary little town. But Riley thought that it was, in fact, just the sort of place where the chain killer might live.

They walked to the door and knocked. A startlingly baby-faced individual answered the door. He was short and extremely thin.

For a second, Riley almost asked, "Is your father at home?" But she stopped herself.

"Are you Wayne Turner," she asked.

"Y-yeah, w-why?" the man stuttered nervously.

Bill took out his badge and said, "We're Agents Jeffreys and Paige, FBI. We'd like to come in and ask you a few questions."

"I-I d-don't understand."

"We'll explain everything," Bill said. "Just let us come in."

Wayne Turner led them into a tidy, modestly decorated living room. With a wordless gesture, he invited Bill and Riley to sit down.

Turner took a long breath to bring his speech under control. Then he said, very slowly but smoothly, "I'm sorry about the stutter. It happens when I'm nervous. I've had a lot of therapy for it. Usually I can control it."

134

Bill said, "Can you tell us where you were last Wednesday night, between dusk and midnight?"

Turner looked uneasy, but managed to control his speech. "I was driving. Between here and Dudley. I was visiting my parents there."

"Can anybody confirm your whereabouts during that time?" Bill asked.

"N-not between the hours you're t-talking about," Turner said, his anxiety mounting. "I-I left my parents' house about eight. I d-didn't get home until almost midnight. It-it's a long drive."

Bill's expression showed increasing suspicion.

He asked, "What about Sunday night? Between eight and ten?"

Turner's eyes darted back and forth.

"Sunday? I-I was at h-h-home," he said.

"Alone?" Bill asked.

"Y-yes."

Riley could see that Turner was starting to panic. But that didn't necessarily mean that he was the man they were looking for. Riley had seen perfectly innocent people get spooked by questions like these. She knew that this interview would go better if she and Bill didn't put him on the defensive. She decided she'd better ask the questions herself.

"We heard that you got a new job," Riley said, not unpleasantly. "Congratulations. Could you tell us about it?"

Turner looked confused, but also a bit flattered. He was able to speak more calmly now.

"I just started working for Decatur Brothers Hardware. A wholesaler. I'm a sales representative. I'll be traveling a lot. I like that. I like to get around."

"And before you got this job?" Riley asked.

Turner lowered his head. She could see she'd touched on a topic that bothered him.

"I-I had trouble getting work for a while," he said. "It's n-not easy when you've g-got a problem talking. It can h-happen at the wrong time."

"I hope this new job works out for you," Riley said.

"Thanks."

Bill put in, "We hear that you got arrested a few months back. Could you tell us about that?"

From Turner's reaction, Riley saw that Bill had touched on an even more difficult subject than employment difficulties. She hoped

135

it wouldn't scuttle the interview altogether.

"Oh, th-that," Turner said, looking quite ashamed. "A woman c-cut in f-front of me in a m-movie line. I c-complained. She m-made fun of me for my st-stutter."

He shook his head.

"I d-don't know what g-got into me," he said. "I h-hit her. I've never d-done anything else like that."

Riley studied his expression. He might be telling the truth, or he might not be. She couldn't be sure.

She said, "Mr. Turner, I hope you don't mind my asking about this. You were adopted, weren't you?"

Turner nodded.

"You said you that you visit your parents in Dudley," Riley said.

Turner took careful control over his voice. "I go there every week," he said.

"So you're on good terms with your parents?" Riley asked.

"Oh, yes," he said. "They've always been good to me."

Riley paused, then said, "You were in an orphanage before you were adopted, weren't you?"

Turner nodded again.

In the gentlest voice possible, Riley asked, "Were you ever mistreated there?"

Turner looked directly into her eyes and spoke with remarkable calm.

"I didn't like it there," he said. "I'd rather not discuss it."

Riley was slightly startled by his sudden composure.

Then Turner asked, "Am I a suspect in some sort of a crime?"

"We're investigating two murders and an abduction," Bill said.

Riley stifled a sigh. Bill's answer wasn't the least bit graceful. Even so, Turner seemed remarkably unperturbed.

"I haven't killed or hurt or abducted anyone," Turner said. "Now if you don't mind, I'm through answering questions. If you need to ask anything else, I'll want my lawyer present."

Bill was about to say something more. Riley silenced him with a gesture.

Turner got up from his chair and walked to his desk. He searched through some cards, then picked one and handed it to Riley.

"Here's my lawyer's card," he said. "Please contact him if you've got any more questions."

Riley smiled politely and said, "We understand, Mr. Turner. Thank you for your time."

Bill and Riley left the house and got into the car.

As Bill started to drive, he said, "Did you hear how his speech changed? He hardly stuttered at all toward the end. What do you make of that?"

Riley didn't reply. The truth was, she wasn't sure what to make of it. The change in Turner's demeanor could well be characteristic of a cold-blooded psychopath. On the other hand, a man who went through life with Turner's speech problem had surely developed more than his share of coping strategies. Perhaps what they'd seen and heard just now showed how strong he was deep down.

As Riley mulled it over, she fingered the card that Turner had given her. Suddenly, something dawned on her.

"Bill, he's not our man," Riley said.

"Why not?"

"Do you remember the business card Lucy told you about? The one the florist gave her?"

Bill nodded. "Yeah, the one that probably has the killer's handwriting."

"It was how he ordered the flowers," Riley said. "He wrote it out by hand. Wayne Turner wouldn't have done that. He'd have talked to the florist, even if it was hard to do. It would be a matter of pride for him. The man we're looking for isn't like that. He can barely talk at all, according to the florist. Some people might actually think that he's mute. Or mentally challenged."

Bill nodded and added, "And he wouldn't be able to get a job as a salesman."

At that moment, Riley's cell phone buzzed. The call was from Lucy.

"Riley, are you making any progress there?"

"No," Riley said. "This wasn't the right guy. We're coming back."

"Oh good," Lucy said, sounding excited. "You'd better get back to Albany as soon as you can."

Riley felt a surge of panic.

"Has something happened with April?" she asked.

"Oh, no, April's fine," Lucy said. "I'm at the field office. I asked one of the hotel cleaning ladies to keep an eye on her. Gave her a pretty big tip for it. April will be okay with this lady."

Riley breathed a sigh of relief. Lucy had probably found a

Hispanic woman, someone who would remind April of Gabriela. It was a smart move.

"So what's going on?" Riley asked.

"Myra Cortese is coming in to the field office," Lucy said. "She's the other nurse who had been with the kidnap victim. She says she's remembering some things."

Chapter 30

Maybe at last we'll get a break, Riley thought. Maybe the nurse had remembered something that would give them some direction, some idea of where to begin looking for Carla Liston. Maybe they would find this very strange chain killer before he murdered the woman he was holding.

When she and Bill got back to the field office, Lucy and Myra Cortese were already waiting for them in a meeting room. The slender, dark-haired woman was not in her nurse's uniform right now. She looked tired. Doubtless she hadn't gotten much sleep since her friend had disappeared. But she also looked eager to help.

"I'm sorry I couldn't tell you anything more when you talked to me last time," Myra said when Bill and Riley sat down at the table. "I was just such a wreck. I was in shock. I couldn't think clearly about anything. I think I can remember more now. At least, some bits and pieces have started coming back to me."

"We appreciate your help, Ms. Cortese," Bill said. "Anything you can remember will be a great help."

Riley could see that Bill was ready to start asking questions. Riley shook her head at him and gestured subtly toward Lucy. Riley preferred that Lucy bring her sensitivity and skill to this interview. Bill understood the message, nodded, and said nothing.

"I'm not sure where to start," Myra said. "I'm remembering details, but I don't know which ones matter. I just thought I should come in and try again."

"That's all right," Lucy said. "We'll talk you through it. Let's start back at the mall. You and Carla were shopping after work, and …"

"Actually, that's not quite right," Myra explained. "We weren't really shopping. There's a little cafe in the mall that we like. We go there most days after we close up the clinic. We just stopped in for some cappuccinos and conversation about anything but work."

Riley felt heartened. She could tell by Myra's tone of voice that she was in a much better frame of mind than she had been during the previous interview.

"Very good, Ms. Cortese," Lucy said. "I hope you don't mind if we ask some of the same questions we asked you before."

"Not at all."

Lucy looked at her with a patient, pleasant expression.

"In the cafe, did you notice anything odd?" Lucy asked. "Any people that stood out? An employee or a customer?"

Myra stopped to think.

"No," she said. "Jenna was the barista as usual. Otherwise, there weren't a lot of people in the cafe. There was an elderly couple at a nearby table. And a woman Carla and I both knew was at another table, a good friend. A young couple … a group of girls … I don't think there was anyone else."

"What time did you leave?" Lucy asked.

"Oh, close to nine, I guess," Myra said. "We walked straight through the mall on the way to the parking lot. It wasn't very far."

Lucy patted the woman's hand.

"On the way through the mall, do you remember anyone who sticks out in your mind?" Lucy asked.

Myra closed her eyes.

"There was a man," she said. "He was tall, heavy, red-haired, had a beard. He made eye contact with me. I think maybe he was leering. I didn't like it."

Riley found all this detail very encouraging. The man she mentioned didn't fit their profile, of course. But if she *had* gotten a good look at the killer, she might remember him and be able to describe him.

"Very good," Lucy said. "And when you went outside?"

"There were just—people, most of them headed toward their cars, like us. There was a bunch of teenagers. Nobody stood out."

The woman's eyes were still closed. Lucy didn't press her with any more questions for a few seconds. Riley understood why. It was best to allow the woman to let her memories float to the surface.

"What about vehicles?" Lucy finally asked. "Just name any that you can remember."

"Well, we were parked next to some kind of low-slung sports car." She paused again, then said, "There was a pickup truck in front of Carla's car. It had a small camper on it. I think there was a big SUV on the other side of us."

Riley started to jot down notes. It wasn't impossible that the killer drove either an SUV or a camper.

Then Myra said, "Oh, and I remember a white van. It backed out just when we did. It was a delivery van, the kind without windows on the sides."

Lucy drew her hand back. She looked shocked.

"Oh my God," Lucy cried.

Riley was startled at Lucy's sudden loss of composure. Myra

140

opened her eyes, surprised as well.

"Is that important?" she asked. "You know, I think that I actually saw a white van again when Carla stopped to let me off. I don't know if it was the same one."

Lucy was searching her cell phone. Then she showed an image to Myra.

"Did it look like this?" she asked.

"Why yes it did," Myra said. "I'm pretty sure the one at the mall looked exactly like that."

Lucy went pale and she trembled a little.

"Myra, you're being a great help," she said, her voice shaky. "Could you wait here a minute while I talk to my colleagues alone?"

"Of course," Myra said.

Lucy got up from her chair. Riley and Bill followed her out of the room.

"Oh my God," Lucy said. "I'm afraid I really screwed up."

"What is it?" Riley said.

Lucy paced back and forth.

"Back in Reedsport, after Rosemary Pickens's funeral, I was walking along and a white van pulled up close to me. Too close, I thought right then."

She showed Bill and Riley the picture on her cell phone.

"Then it sped up and drove away, and I snapped this picture. It was kind of automatic, but you can see I didn't get the license number. I didn't give it another thought—until just now. It must have been him. I missed him. I let him get away."

Riley felt a surge of disappointment. It was the first really foolish thing she'd known Lucy to do. But Bill didn't seem to feel that way.

"Take it easy," he said to Lucy. "We're still not sure the van you saw is the one Myra remembered. There are lots of white vans out there. It could be just a coincidence."

Riley doubted that very much. Judging from her anguished expression, so did Lucy.

"I've got to fix this," Lucy said. "I've got to make this right. I have to go talk to Paul, the technician. He can contact the mall, check their security photos."

*

141

A little while after they had thanked Myra Cortese for being helpful and let her go home, Riley, Bill, and Lucy were in the lab, waiting to see what Paul Nooney could turn up. Right away he had told them that the van in Lucy's photograph was a Ford, about ten years old. It had no letters on the side or any other identification, although the paint was definitely scratched.

Now the computer tech was searching mall security camera images for a match.

"Got it," Paul said. "Have a look."

Riley huddled with Bill and Lucy behind Paul. Sure enough, the camera had caught the back of a white Ford delivery van pulling out of the mall parking lot.

"How can we be sure it's the same vehicle?" Bill asked.

Lucy held the picture on her cell phone next to the image on the computer.

"Right there—you can see where the paint is scratched in the same place. It's the same van, all right. I really did screw up. But at least we've got a clear shot of the plate. It's a Pennsylvania plate. Paul, how fast do you think you can track down the owner?"

"Give me just a minute," Paul said. He got back to work.

Riley took Bill by the elbow and led him a short distance away from Lucy.

"I'm so disappointed in her, Bill," Riley said quietly so that Lucy couldn't hear. "I thought she was better than this."

"Come on, Riley," Bill said. "Don't try to tell me you didn't make your own share of screw-ups when you were a rookie. I sure as hell did. And even if she dropped the ball at first, she didn't forget completely. She came through in the end."

Riley knew that Bill was right. He almost always was, and sometimes that pissed her off. She turned and saw that Lucy was looking miserable.

Riley walked over to the young agent and said, "It's okay."

"No, it's not," Lucy said.

Just then Paul called out.

"Here it is. Come here and let me show you."

They all gathered behind Paul and looked over his shoulder. The security photo was still on the screen, next to some DMV documents.

"The registration is way out of date," he said. "It's been expired for years. The date sticker in the photo looks current, but I suspect it's a phony. The name and address on the registration also turns up in driver's licenses. He's still at the same location. His name is Walter Sattler, and he still lives in Hoxeyville, Pennsylvania. That's just over the state line, only a couple of hours from here."

The driver's license photo showed a thin, boyish face. The man was five feet seven inches tall. He was thirty-three.

"That's got to be him," Bill said. "Let's get a warrant and go."

Riley nodded.

"We might still have time to save Carla."

Chapter 31

Riley thought that maybe this long day would end in success after all. Starting with the trip to Sing Sing, the bits and pieces that had come together pointed to this address in Hoxeyville, Pennsylvania. She and Bill approached the house cautiously.

It had taken longer than they'd expected to get a search warrant and the drive had been a couple of hours, so it was now very late and very dark. The modest working-class neighborhood seemed pleasant and peaceful. Although no lights were on inside or outside the house, the street was well lighted. Riley could see that the house had basement windows—just the place where someone might be held captive. Although no vehicle was parked near the house there was a closed-up garage. The van was probably in there.

"Weapons?" Riley asked quietly, getting ready to pull her Glock. They had decided that the captive might stand a better chance of survival if they didn't storm the place with a SWAT team.

"Not yet," Bill said. "With luck we won't need them. He's not a shooter and not very strong."

As they stepped up onto the front porch, Riley hoped he was right. Still, she hadn't dealt with many cold-blooded murderers who hadn't put up some resistance. And most of them were armed.

Bill pushed the doorbell and also knocked sharply on the front door. No reply came for a few moments. Bill knocked again.

"FBI," Bill called out. "Is this the residence of Walter Sattler? We've got a warrant."

Again there was no reply, but Riley thought that she heard movement behind the door. Instinctively, she drew her pistol in spite of Bill's reluctance to use guns.

Suddenly the door swung open. A smallish man wearing pajamas stood inside, pointing a shotgun at them. Riley leveled her Glock at his face.

"Put the weapon down," Bill barked, drawing his own pistol.

"Easy," the man said, swinging the gun barrel back and forth between Riley and Bill. "Take it easy. I don't want any trouble. I just want to see badges."

With their free hands, Bill and Riley displayed their badges. The man lowered his weapon.

"Put the gun down," Bill said again.

"Okay. Jesus." The man stooped down and put the weapon on

144

the floor. Riley picked it up.

"Hands on your head," Bill said.

The man complied. "I'm cooperating," he said. "What's this all about?"

Riley's heart sank.

He can talk just fine, she thought. The man sounded as nervous as anyone might be in this situation, but there was no trace of a stutter.

Still, she recognized the man whose picture they'd seen on the driver's license. This was definitely Walter Sattler. There had to be a reason the evidence had led to him.

Could they be dealing with two perpetrators working as a team?

But no, that didn't fit.

Riley was getting ready to holster her weapon when a woman's voice snapped her back to attention.

"Walter, what's going on? Should I call 911?"

The woman was standing at the top of the stairs in her nightgown. She had curlers in her hair.

"No, you don't have to do that, Peg," Walter Sattler said. "It's the FBI. I don't know what they want. Just check and make sure the kids aren't scared. Go back to bed. I'll handle this."

The woman went back upstairs. Sattler was still holding his hands where they could be clearly seen.

Bill quickly patted him down for other possible weapons. Finding nothing, he holstered his pistol, but Riley kept hers drawn.

"We've got a warrant to search the place," Bill said, producing the document.

"What if I don't want you to?" Sattler said.

Riley said, "You can take that up with your lawyer later on." Turning to Bill, she said, "The basement seems the most likely."

Bill walked back through the house and disappeared.

"What's all this about?" Sattler asked Riley. "What are you looking for, anyhow?"

"Do you own a white Ford delivery van?"

Sattler looked completely taken aback.

"What? No! We've got a Nissan station wagon. It's back in the garage. Why, I haven't had a Ford since …"

His voice trailed off. He seemed to be remembering something. Bill came back into the room.

"Nothing suspicious in the basement," Bill said. "Should I

145

check the attic?"

"No," Riley said. "Hold off a few minutes."

With a wife and kid upstairs, she knew that it wasn't likely that the missing woman was a prisoner here. It seemed pretty obvious by now that Sattler wasn't keeping anyone captive, at least not in this house.

Sattler's demeanor was much more docile than before.

"Look, there's been a misunderstanding," he said. "Sit down. I think maybe we can sort this out."

Riley and Bill sat down with him in the living room.

"Tell me more about this Ford van you're talking about," Sattler said.

"I'll show it to you," Riley said.

On her cell phone, she brought up the photo that Lucy had taken, alongside the security photo. She showed it to Sattler.

"Damn it," Sattler growled. "I thought I'd seen the last of that van."

"Please explain this to us, Mr. Sattler," Riley said.

Sattler took a long, slow breath.

"Look, the guy you're looking for isn't me," he said. "You're looking for my cousin, Eugene Fisk. I haven't seen him for years. What has he done?"

"He's a suspect in two murders and an abduction," Bill said.

Sattler's mouth dropped open with shock.

Riley asked, "How did he wind up with your van?"

"I gave it to him nine years ago," Sattler said. "I wanted him gone so badly, I didn't bother to transfer the ownership. I just handed him the keys and said, 'Drive away from here and don't let me ever see or hear from you again.' That's what he did."

Sattler hung his head guiltily.

"I know it wasn't the right thing to do," he said. "I've had second thoughts about it ever since. But if you knew Eugene … Well, I just wanted him out of my life for good."

Sattler stared across the room with an expression of shame and regret.

"What can you tell us about him?" Riley asked.

"Eugene was my mother's sister's kid," Sattler said. "Her name was Sherry Fisk. I never really knew her. The whole family—my parents included—thought she was just trailer trash. Folks also said she was crazy."

Sattler paused for a moment.

146

"Nobody knew who Eugene's father was," he said. "And I never really got to know Eugene—at least not as a kid. His mother was murdered when I a teenager. Eugene was ten, I think. I never heard the details, how it happened. It was one of those family secrets nobody wanted to talk about. They never caught the killer."

Riley was taking notes.

"What happened to Eugene after his mother was killed?" she asked.

"I think he was in a foster home," Sattler said. "He got into some kind of trouble, and he wound up institutionalized for mental problems."

Sattler paused again.

"They let him out when he was eighteen. I was in my twenties, married, getting a pretty good start in life. Like I said, I never really knew him when we were kids. But now suddenly he acted like we'd always been close. And he was …"

Sattler shook his head.

"Well, he was weird, that's all. He could barely talk at all. It was so bad he'd sometimes write notes to you instead of saying anything. And he was needy. He was always hitting me up for money, hanging around for meals. It wasn't just awkward. It was scary. It was almost like stalking. I just had this feeling when he was around …"

His voice trailed off again.

"Anyway," he said, "that was when I gave him the van. And told him never to come back."

Riley took a moment to mull over what she'd just learned. Maybe there was someone in Hoxeyville who might be able to tell them more about Eugene Fisk.

"Are your parents alive?" she asked Sattler.

"No, I'm the last of the family. Except for Eugene."

"Where was Eugene institutionalized?"

"It was at the Hoxeyville Psychiatric Center, right here in town."

Riley figured that would be their next stop. Surely they'd be able to learn more there. But maybe she could get one other thing from Sattler.

"Do you have any pictures of your cousin?" she asked.

"None that would show how he looks now," Sattler said. "But I think I've got an old one …"

He got up from his chair and opened a drawer. He rummaged

around inside until he found a snapshot. He handed it to Riley.

"This one was taken when we were just kids," he said. "I kept it because it was pretty unusual for us to get together."

While Bill asked a few final questions, Riley stared at the photo. It showed two young boys. The taller one was recognizably Sattler. The shorter one was an odd-looking child, his features somewhat exaggerated.

Even so, Riley couldn't help thinking …

What a sweet smile he has!

She couldn't imagine what had turned that smiling little boy into a serial killer.

Chapter 32

Carla had no idea how long she'd been chained on the cot in this basement. The windows high up on the cinderblock walls were covered with cardboard, sealing out every trace of outdoor light. Whenever the overhead light was off, which it was right now, she was in complete darkness.

She did know that she was hungry, soiled, and in terrible pain. She'd had nothing to eat during the whole time she'd been here. Sometimes the monstrous little man would loosen the chain gag from her mouth and give her a sip of water, and that was all.

She'd long since stopped being bothered by her own stench. Her dignity no longer mattered to her. Her survival did.

But so far, escape had eluded her.

He'd cudgeled her with a chain when he first took her back in Albany. Now that the delirium from her concussion had passed, she was dazed and bewildered from pain and hunger. She'd sleep or pass out from time to time, then wake up with no idea where she was or what had happened.

But she always managed to bring herself back to her horrible present reality. Clear-headedness was essential. There was a way out, she was sure of it. She thrashed a little in the darkness, rolling her body back and forth. She'd been doing that all along, whenever he wasn't here. He'd wrapped the chains around her and the cot, but they apparently weren't really fastened. Little by little, she had felt them loosening.

Right now she guessed that they hung loosely enough for her to try to slip out of them. The straitjacket was yet another problem, but she'd deal with that afterward.

Starting with her shoulders, she wiggled and squirmed so that the chains began to slip.

But then she heard his footsteps. He was probably on his way down here. Now was no time to struggle with the chains. She let her exhausted body go limp.

She heard the door open at the top of the flight of stairs that led from the house down into the basement. Then she was blinded by the overhead light. She shut her eyes, pretending to be asleep. She listened to the sound of his footsteps coming down the stairs.

In a moment, she could hear his breathing as he leaned over her. She could feel that he was fingering the chains. As he often did, he started whispering to them—whispering so quietly that she

149

couldn't make out his words. It was as if she weren't here at all, and the chains were the only living things in the basement.

As a nurse, she'd dealt in the past with psychotic patients. This man was seriously mentally ill, and she knew it. He'd often go over to his worktable and stretch out other chains that he kept there. He'd carry on long conversations with them, sometimes pleading with them, sometimes swearing his loyalty to them, sometimes assuring them that everything was going as they wished.

When he tried to say anything to her, he was always wracked by a hopeless stammer. But he could always talk perfectly to the chains.

She breathed slowly and regularly, as if asleep. After a while, she heard his footsteps going back up the stairs and through the house. She heard the front door open and close. She opened her eyes. It was pitch dark again.

She listened closely. She couldn't hear any more footsteps above her. That must mean that he had left. Sometimes he went away completely for hours at a time, and that's what she was hoping for now.

Her whole body screamed with pain as she began to wriggle and writhe again. Like a moth struggling to emerge from a cocoon, she managed to make the coil of chains slip down along her abdomen. Soon she was free of them all the way down to her waist.

Struggling against the straitjacket, she managed to sit up. For a moment she was seized by dizziness and she nearly fainted. But she recovered and shook and wiggled her legs until the chains slipped down to her ankles. She tucked up her knees and pulled her feet free.

She was sitting on the edge of the cot, still bound by the straitjacket. Now it was time to deal with that problem. She'd been thinking about how to get out of it for as long as she'd been down here. She'd been unconscious when he'd put it on her, but he must to have done it in a hurry because he hadn't pulled it very tight.

She remembered seeing an escape artist on television demonstrating how to get out of a straitjacket. In her mind, she carefully went over the steps he'd used.

I can do that, she thought. *I will do it.*

First she relaxed and exhaled, making her body as small as possible. The straitjacket felt looser. Then she swung her outer arm toward the opposite shoulder. From that position, it wasn't hard to lift the arm up and pull the restraining strap over her head and to the front of her body. She raised the buckle on her sleeve to her face, then opened it with her teeth. Then she did the same with the other arm.

Now her hands were completely free. It was easy to unfasten the remaining buckles, stand up, and slip out of the straitjacket altogether.

But free as she was, the pain was greater than ever, and she dropped back down onto the cot. Muscles that hadn't been used in days were now in agony, and parts of her body were numb from the lack of blood flow.

She shook herself all over, then mustered up all her willpower and forced herself to stand again. She knew that there was a basement door that led outside. There was also a stairway up into the house. The man who held her had come in and out both ways.

Groping with feet and hands, she found her way to the back door. She fumbled around until she found the doorknob. She turned the lock on the doorknob and twisted it. The door didn't come open. She felt around above the doorknob and realized that she couldn't open it without a key.

For a few long moments, Carla felt like giving up. To get out of the basement, she would have to go up through the house. She finally mustered up her courage to do that. She really had no other option.

Dark as the basement was, she had a fair idea of how to get to the stairs. She staggered around until she found the banister and the bottom step. Step by step, she moved upward as silently as she could. When she reached the door at the top, it wasn't locked.

Carla pushed the door open and stepped out into the killer's house. The cramped and dingy living area was silent. The killer must not be there.

Carla's weakness almost caught up with her then. She hadn't eaten for days and dizziness nearly overcame her. But she gathered her resolve and moved across the little living room to the front door.

When she opened the door, she looked outside into the dim light of day. She couldn't tell whether it was early morning or evening. A white van was in the driveway—the same van the man had used to capture her. Beyond that, she saw another house just a short way down the road that ran by the house.

That's where I have to go, she told herself.

But just as she moved in that direction, the nightmarish little man appeared from the other side of the van. He must have been

151

puttering around back there, and now he stepped out just in time to see her. He was holding a bundle of heavy chains in one hand when their eyes met. She opened her mouth and tried to scream, but nothing came out.

She turned back into the house and tried to slam the door to shut the man out, but he was too fast. He pushed his way inside.

Carla called on all her resources now. Despite her pain or dizziness, she seized on whatever she could find to throw at him. She overturned a small table in his path. He dodged the table and came relentlessly toward her.

She backed into the tiny kitchen and snatched up a heavy pan from a countertop. She swung it hard into the side of his head, and he dropped to his knees.

She looked at him and sized him up, and she realized with a shock that she was more stout than he was. He was practically puny.

Carla had never hurt anyone in her life, but now a primal instinct kicked in. She found her body flooded with rage, and she leapt atop her would-be killer. She tackled him to the ground, and was amazed to find herself stronger than he was. She landed on top of him and raised her fists and punched him in the face, again and again.

The killer tried to fight back, but he couldn't overpower her. Instead, he whimpered like a little boy.

Finally, his face a bloody mess, he stopped moving.

Carla looked down, stunned. She also felt the room spin, and as she reeled herself, she realized how weak and dizzy she was.

She jumped off him, not wanting to touch him or be anywhere near him. She spit down on his face, stepped over him, and walked for the open door with a rush of relief.

Suddenly, Carla couldn't breathe. She couldn't understand what was happening, until she heard him behind her and she reached up and felt a length of chain wrapped around her throat. She struggled and kicked, but this time, he was too strong.

And in another few seconds, the world went completely dark.

*

Eugene dragged the woman by the neck back to the basement door. She was unconscious and heavy, and she fell down the steps. When he followed her down and looked closely, he realized that she was dead. He had broken her neck by dragging her that way.

"Oh, no," he gasped.

Tears of grief and panic sprung to his eyes. This wasn't the way it was supposed to happen. He'd expected to keep her alive another week at least.

He opened the back door, switched on the basement light, and pushed the body down the stairs. He saw where the chains that had bound the woman lay all around the cot. They were angry with him. He knew it. He had let them down.

He thought maybe he could mollify them with a familiar gesture—by doing what he'd done to kill the other women. So he picked up his straight-edged razor and slit her lifeless throat. But it was no good. He couldn't pretend that he'd done what the chains demanded.

Now he would have to take her back to where he'd captured her, displaying her for the world to see. After that he needed to find a new victim, and quickly. The chains would make his life hell until he did.

Chapter 33

Checking into the motel had been rather tense.

"Do you want separate rooms?" the woman at the desk had asked.

Bill had actually turned to Riley, as if waiting for her response. She hadn't reacted at all, so he'd told the woman, *"Yes."*

It was morning now, and they were on the road. Riley was wondering what would have happened if she'd nodded her approval at that critical moment. What might last night have been like?

This morning they weren't discussing that question or much of anything else. They'd barely even said a word to each other over breakfast back at the motel. They'd scarcely talked at all on the drive to the Hoxeyville Psychiatric Center where Eugene Fisk had spent a large part of his life.

Riley had called the hospital earlier this morning. She'd been surprised that Eugene's supervising physician seemed perfectly happy to meet with them. Physicians normally balked at this kind of interview because of physician-patient privilege. For some reason, Dr. Joseph Lombard didn't seem concerned about that, and she was eager to find out why.

Steady, she thought as the hospital building came into view. *This is no time to think about last night.*

After all, Bill was desperately trying to patch things up with Maggie, and Riley had a swarm of personal issues to deal with. They also had work to do, and their formerly solid rapport was shaky already.

Still, she couldn't help wondering about that drunken suggestion she'd made to Bill over the phone, the one that had all but ruined their friendship. Had he really been offended by it, or had he been scared instead? Scared that something was almost sure to happen between them sooner or later? Was the possibility still in the air?

She glanced sideways at Bill. He looked every bit the well-disciplined FBI agent that he was, with his dark hair carefully combed. In fact, he'd made a greater effort than usual to look professional. He didn't always wear a suit and a tie. At the moment, he seemed to be completely focused on his driving, but she couldn't help but wonder if he was asking himself questions similar to hers. His strong face gave her no clue.

Riley put all such thoughts aside as Bill parked in the visitors'

154

lot. They walked into the hospital, checked in, and were escorted directly to Dr. Lombard's office.

The doctor, a tall man of about sixty, rose from his desk to meet them.

"Agents Paige and Jeffreys, I presume," he said. "Please sit down."

Bill and Riley sat down in the chairs in front of the doctor's desk. For a moment the doctor stood looking at them with an anxious expression.

"You said that you want to talk to me about Eugene Fisk," he said. "He was in our care about ten years back."

The doctor sat down and continued. "When you called you mentioned that you were in Pennsylvania searching for information about a murderer over in New York. You mentioned chains, straitjackets, slit throats. And you said that there's another captive? Horrible."

He paused for a moment.

"Am I correct in understanding that Mr. Fisk is a suspect?" he asked.

"He's our only suspect," Bill said.

Dr. Lombard didn't reply, but his expression was one of deep concern.

Riley said, "Dr. Lombard, as I stressed to you, information is urgent. We appreciate your willingness to talk to us about Mr. Fisk without a warrant."

"Yes, I'm sure that's unusual," Lombard replied. "But Pennsylvania law is quite specific about the matter. I'm only forbidden to exchange medical information that 'blackens' my patient's character."

Dr. Lombard gazed significantly at Riley, then at Bill.

"I'll make sure not to cross that line," he said.

Riley understood. The doctor was eager to cooperate. But this was not going to be a typical interview. What went unsaid was likely to be as important as what was said. Riley knew that she had to be alert to unspoken clues.

The doctor opened a file.

"I've got his records right here," he said, glancing over its contents. "He was admitted here sixteen years ago. He was eleven years old. He was an orphan, and he'd been living in a group foster home that had just burned down. He was ... deeply traumatized afterwards."

155

The doctor stopped. Riley detected that he was leaving a great deal unsaid.

She said, "We understand that he stayed under your care until he was eighteen."

"That's right," Lombard said. "When he first came here, he was barely communicative at all. He stayed huddled up and ignored anyone who tried to talk to him. But little by little, he improved. He came out of his shell."

The doctor knitted his brow, remembering.

"He had a terrible speech problem," he said. "Never got rid of it, even after he started getting better. I'm sure that he'd had it from early childhood. He could talk to *me* just a little. But often he'd write down what he wanted to say instead of trying to speak."

Lombard leaned back in his chair.

"He made slow but excellent progress," he said. "Or so I'd thought. He learned a lot while he was here. He learned to garden, how to use a computer, took some classes. He was extremely good-natured, generous, kind. He was never the least bit aggressive. Everybody liked him—other patients, the personnel. I liked him."

He pulled a photograph from the file and passed it over to them. The teenager had a warm smile, but Riley thought his eyes looked rather blank.

The doctor continued, but a tone of regret was starting to creep into his voice.

"He seemed more than ready to go out into the world. We released him. We tried to keep track of his whereabouts and activities. But soon he disappeared completely. I worried about that. It was nine years ago."

The doctor's voice trailed off. Riley knew that she was going to have to coax more information out of him.

She said, "Dr. Lombard, we're going to ask you a few questions. If you can legally answer them, please do so. If you can't, you don't have to say anything. Does that sound okay with you?"

"That sounds fine," the doctor said.

Riley glanced at Bill. He nodded. Riley could see that he understood this tactic and was ready to join in.

"Dr. Lombard," Riley said, "when Eugene's foster home burned down, was arson ever suspected?"

The doctor stared ahead fixedly and said nothing.

Bill put in, "Did anybody die in the incident?"

Again, the doctor said nothing.

Riley asked, "Was somebody murdered?"

The doctor looked at her without saying a word.

Finally he said, "I think that's all I can tell you."

Bill said, "Maybe you could help with one more thing. Has the foster home been rebuilt? Is it operating now?"

"It is," Lombard said. "I'll give you the address."

Lombard wrote down the address and handed it to Bill.

Riley looked again at the photograph of Eugene Fisk. "Could you give us a copy of this?" she asked.

"You can keep that one. I'll print another for the file."

Bill and Riley both thanked him for his help and left his office.

"That was informative," Bill said as they headed for the car. "Let's head right over to that foster home."

Riley said, "While you drive, I'll call Sam Flores back in Quantico. I'll get him to look for news stories about what happened at the orphanage."

*

The St. Genesius Children's Home was located in Bowerbank, Pennsylvania, about a half hour from Hoxeyville. While Bill was driving, Riley received a newspaper article from Sam Flores. What she read chilled her to the bone.

Sixteen years ago, the group foster home was burned to the ground. Arson was suspected. The body of a twelve-year-old boy, Ethan Holbrook, had been found in the ruins. The article didn't specify the cause of death.

"That poor kid could have been Eugene's first victim," Riley said after she'd finished reading the article to Bill.

"Jesus," Bill murmured. "He started as a pre-teen? What kind of monster are we dealing with?"

Riley remembered Dr. Lombard's stony silence when she'd asked him if someone had been murdered. She thought about the smiling young child she'd seen in the photograph at Walter Sattler's house. How soon had that child been turned into a killer?

When Bill parked the car, Riley observed that the group home was housed in a clean, modern building. Outside in front was a playground with colorful equipment. There were dozens of kids playing happily.

Two gray-clad, smiling nuns were watching over them. Riley

and Bill approached the closest one.

"Excuse me, Sister," Riley said. "Could you take us to this facility's director?"

"That would be me," the nun said pleasantly. "Sister Cecilia Berry. What can I do for you?"

Riley was surprised at how young she looked. It didn't seem likely that she'd been in charge of this place all those years ago. Riley wondered what they could hope to learn from her.

Riley and Bill both took out their badges.

"We're Agents Jeffreys and Paige, FBI," Bill said. "We'd like to ask you a few questions."

Sister Cecilia's smile dropped away. She turned pale. She looked around, as if to make sure that nobody was watching.

"Please come with me," she said. She called to another nun to take over the playground supervision.

Riley and Bill walked with her into the building. On their way to nun's office, Riley noticed that the building was organized like a dormitory. Down one hall, she saw rows of rooms, many with their doors open. A couple of kindly-looking nuns were checking in on the kids, stopping to talk with them as they went. Music, conversation, and laughter could be heard.

From what Riley could see, the St. Genesius Children's Home was a warm, welcoming place.

So why is this woman so uneasy? Riley wondered.

Riley and Bill sat down in Sister Cecilia's office. But the sister didn't sit down. She paced with agitation.

"I don't know why you're here," she said. "We've had no complaints since this new facility opened. We have lawyers to deal with the old cases. If you've checked with the DHS, they'll tell you that we pass every inspection with a perfect score. I'll show you the latest report."

She started to open a file drawer.

"Sister Cecilia, I don't think you understand the nature of our visit," Bill said.

Riley added, "We're here to ask about a child who was here sixteen years ago. Eugene Fisk. We're trying to find him. He's the subject of a murder investigation."

"Oh," the sister said with surprise. She sat behind her desk.

"Please excuse my mistake," she said. "We're trying to put our history behind us. I'm sure you can understand."

The truth was, Riley didn't understand, and she was sure that

Bill didn't either.

"What can you tell us about Eugene Fisk?" Riley asked.

Sister Cecilia looked wary.

"What do you know already?" she asked.

Bill said, "We know that he was transferred to a psychiatric hospital after your old facility burned down. A boy died in that fire—Ethan Holbrook. We're here to find out more about what happened."

"It was before my time, of course," Sister Cecilia said, getting up from her desk and going back to the file cabinet. "But I know Eugene's story well."

She opened a drawer, took out a file, and sat down again.

"It was a terrible story," she said, opening the file and scanning its contents. "Most of the nuns thought Eugene had started the fire. They even thought he might have killed Ethan. Nothing was ever proven."

"Why would he have killed another child?" Riley asked.

Referring to the old file, Sister Cecilia explained, "It seemed that Ethan Holbrook was an awful bully. He was particularly ugly toward Eugene. Eugene was small, weak, and awkward. And he had a terrible speech impediment. Ethan tormented and mocked him about it."

"Why didn't the nuns put a stop to the bullying?" Riley asked.

Sister Cecilia fell silent.

"I get the impression there's something you don't want to tell us," Riley said.

Slowly and reluctantly, the sister said, "There's quite a lot I'd rather not tell you, actually. It's not exactly a secret. It's not a secret at all. You can find court records about it, and old news stories. It's just so awful to have to dredge up the past. And I'd hate to have it all in the news again. With the Lord's help, we've tried to put it all behind us. We do nothing but good work here now. We really do."

"We're sure that's true," Riley said. "But it would help if you'd tell us."

Sister Cecilia said nothing for a moment. Then she continued, "After the fire, when the home was just starting to be rebuilt, the truth began to come out. The director back then was Sister Veronica Orlando. She'd run the place for more than a decade. She and her nuns were merciless. They encouraged the kids to bully each other. And she and the nuns would punish kids horribly for the smallest things—like sneezing or wetting the bed."

159

Riley was struck by the sister's sad expression. She could see that Sister Cecilia was doing her best to redeem the home from its awful history. Even so, the poor woman couldn't help but be haunted by a past for which she had no responsibility.

"Sister Cecilia," Riley asked in a gentle tone, "did any of these punishments involve chains?"

"If you're asking whether the kids themselves were chained up, no," she said. "But Sister Veronica and her nuns did sometimes lock them up by putting chains on the doors."

Sister Cecilia tilted her head inquisitively.

"But it's interesting you should ask about chains," she said, checking the record again. "Eugene came here when he was ten years old. He'd been found with a shackle on one ankle, chained to a post in his house. He was starving, and he couldn't talk at all."

"Where was his mother?" Bill asked.

"She'd been murdered. Her body was found right there in the house, right in front of the child where he would have seen the whole thing. The killer was never caught."

"How was she killed?" Riley asked.

"Her throat was slit," Sister Cecilia said. "The straight razor that killed her was found there too, thrown down on the floor near her. But they didn't find any prints on it."

Then the nun looked out the window, still with that haunted expression.

"The newspapers didn't say it," she said, "but that was how Ethan Holbrook died, too."

Chapter 34

Riley was awakened by Lucy charging through the door between their adjoining hotel rooms.

"Turn on your TV!" Lucy cried.

Riley yanked herself to a sitting position. "What?" she asked. She saw that it was morning. She and Bill had gotten back to Albany last night. In the other bed, April growled sleepily, "What's going on?"

"I'll get it," Lucy said. She found the clicker and turned the television on herself. The first words Riley heard were those of a news announcer.

"We must warn our viewers that some of the images you're about to see are graphic."

Riley immediately saw that the announcer really meant it. The first image was of a chain-bound body dangling from a tree branch. Mercifully, the body was facing away from the camera.

The announcer continued, "A woman was brutally murdered last night, her body left in Albany's Curtis Park. This seems to be the latest in a series of 'chain murders' that have terrorized the Hudson River area over the last five years. The victim's identity is being withheld pending notification of her family …"

"No," Riley muttered. "It can't be. Not yet."

The tree branch overhung a road, and it looked like the same park where Carla Liston had been abducted. The hanging body surely must be that of Carla Liston. But it was too soon. He'd only taken her a few days ago.

As the announcer continued, the camera panned to show that a small crowd of gawkers had clustered just outside the area that the cops had taped off. The whole situation was an investigator's nightmare.

Now the on-the-scene reporter was talking to the man who had discovered the body a couple of hours earlier.

"I was just driving through the park on my way to work," the man said. "When I saw it, I almost wrecked my car. Then I thought maybe it was a dummy hung up by some sick pranksters. But when you look you can tell …"

At that moment came a sharp knock on the hotel room door. While Riley stared at the TV screen, Lucy went to the door and let Bill in.

He said, "I just got a call from Harvey Dewhurst, the head of

161

the Albany field office. He's going out of his mind. That guy you see on camera there called the media before he called the police."

Riley shook her head wearily. "Well, he's sure getting his fifteen minutes of fame," she said.

Bill continued, "As soon as the police heard about it, they knew it was our case and called the field office. But by the time Dewhurst and his people got there, the media was all over the scene. And the sightseers had also started to arrive."

"We have to get over there," Lucy said.

Riley was already out of bed, scrounging around for clothes. She carried her things into the bathroom and got dressed in a hurry. No time for breakfast, she knew. Maybe they could grab some coffee when they went by the motel breakfast room.

When she came out, Bill and Lucy were waiting by the door.

"We've got to go, April," Riley said to her daughter. "All of us. You stay put right here."

"It's your job," April said. "Go. I'll be fine."

*

During the drive to Curtis Park, Riley was still trying to get her mind around what had happened.

"I don't get what's going on," she said. "He's breaking his own MO. He's supposed to hold his victims captive for a longer time. For weeks. Why did he kill her so fast?"

A wave of discouragement swept over her.

"I thought we had more time to find Carla Liston," she added sadly.

"We did everything we could," Lucy said from the back seat.

But Bill said nothing as he drove. Riley knew that he felt exactly the same as she did. After all their years doing this job, they'd never gotten used to losing a victim. It was especially hard when they felt that they were closing in on the killer.

When they arrived at the park, Riley saw that television crew vans were mingled with police vehicles. The crowd outside the taped-off area had gotten larger, and people were snapping pictures with their cell phones. She and Lucy followed Bill as he pushed his way through to the police tape. They showed their badges to a pair of cops who were doing their best to control the area.

Then the three of them walked up the road toward where the body was still hanging in plain view. Riley could now see that the

162

victim was clad in a straitjacket, just the same as the earlier victims. And like Rosemary Pickens in Reedsport, she'd been hauled up on a rope that ran through a pulley.

Riley stopped and stared, shaken by the sheer audacity of the display. Eugene Fisk must have stopped his van here before dawn, climbed up onto the overhanging limb, fastened the pulley in place, then climbed back down and hoisted Carla Liston's body.

And all without being seen, Riley thought. He'd been more than daring, but he'd also been lucky.

This wasn't some abandoned warehouse by a railroad track, but a well-used road through a city park. With any other serial killer, Riley would assume that he was becoming more brazen, thumbing his nose at the authorities. But she knew that Eugene Fisk was a different sort of creature. This was more likely to be a gesture of sheer desperation. Again she wondered what was going on with the maniacal killer.

Special Agent Harvey Dewhurst trotted toward them. He was overweight and middle-aged, and at the moment he was anxious, red-faced, and sweating. He was also as angry as hell.

"I hate it when this kind of shit happens," Dewhurst said. "You guys are the Quantico experts. You tell me what we can do for damage control."

"First of all, you'd better get her down," Bill said.

Riley agreed. She had asked Chief Alford to leave Rosemary Pickens's body hanging until she could get to the scene, but this was a different matter. The Reedsport police had been in better control of the crime scene. Here, too many pictures had been taken of this corpse already. And she and the rest of the FBI on site had already looked everything over.

Dewhurst turned to the local cop in charge.

"Tell your people to bring her down," he said. "And tell the coroner to get right to work on the body." He looked around and added, "And clear those onlookers out of here. Move the tape back where they can't take pictures and open up some room for the coroner to get his wagon in."

The cop hurried away to carry out Dewhurst's orders.

"What next?" Dewhurst asked.

Riley thought for a moment.

"We might as well take advantage of the media," she said. "Have the local TV stations alert the public that we're looking for a white Ford delivery van. A dented rear bumper, no other known markings, a Pennsylvania license plate. Agent Vargas can give you a photo that she took of it. Make sure the public sees it."

Then Riley reached into her bag and pulled out the photo of Eugene that the psychiatrist had given her.

"This picture shows the suspect as a teenager," Riley explained. "He's now twenty-seven years old. Take this back to the field office and run it through the age progression program. We should be able to get a good image of what he probably looks like now. Then make sure it gets on TV and the Internet."

She thought another moment and said, "Don't mention that the perp has a stutter. That will help filter the calls."

At that moment the coroner called out to Dewhurst, "You'd better have a look at something over here." He was crouched over the body that had been lowered carefully to the ground.

Riley, Bill, and Lucy all followed Dewhurst to see what the coroner was indicating. The woman's eyes were wide open, and she still wore a terrified expression on her face. The coroner pointed to her throat.

"Her throat was slit," he said, "and it's my understanding that's how he finished off the other victims. But look here. There wasn't much bleeding at all."

He turned and looked at them. "It wasn't the cause of death. This time, her neck was broken first."

Bill looked at Riley with surprise.

"Another change from his MO," he said to her. "What's going on with this guy?"

"I don't know why he's changing so fast," Riley said. "He doesn't seem like the type who would change at all. But I do know who we should ask about it."

Chapter 35

Riley was once again inside Sing Sing Correctional Facility. She hoped this turned out to be a good idea. Bill was with her, although he had joined her only reluctantly, insisting it was a detour from their investigation. But deep in her gut, Riley felt that Shane Hatcher would still have valuable insights to share.

"I sure hope you're right about this," Bill grumbled as the guard led them into the visiting room—the same cream-colored room where Riley had met with Shane Hatcher two days ago.

As soon as they sat down at the table, Hatcher was escorted into the room by a pair of guards. He sat down across from them, and for a long moment he stared over the top of his reading glasses at Bill. Then he turned to Riley.

"I see you brought a friend with you," he told her.

"This is Special Agent Bill Jeffreys, from Quantico," Riley said. "He's come to Albany to join in the investigation."

Hatcher sat there with that now-familiar inscrutable smile on his hardened face. Again, he looked Bill over the way he'd looked at Riley the last time—sizing him up, figuring out what made him tick.

Riley knew that in spite of—or perhaps because of—being locked up for a long time, Hatcher was a cunning observer of human nature. She wondered what kinds of observations he was making about Bill right now.

"You don't need to tell me why you're here," Hatcher said. "I saw it all on TV. Quite a scene. I figured you'd be back."

He shook his head with disapproval.

"All those vultures out there—reporters, gawkers, TV executives crazed for ratings. Doesn't it make you crazy? One thing about this place, you don't have to deal with that kind of barbarity. Sure, we've got our own various kinds of barbarity, but really, I prefer it. It's like I tell everybody here, freedom is overrated. Do they believe me? Never."

Riley heard Bill's derisive snort. She found it a bit weird herself to hear this kind of moralizing from a multiple murderer. But she reminded herself that Shane Hatcher was no ordinary monster. She thought that even if she were to talk to him every single day for years on end, he'd always be able to surprise her—and probably also to scare her.

"You were right about everything," Riley said. "The

perpetrator was tormented as a kid. His mother chained him up, he was bullied in an orphanage—bullied by other kids, and also by the nuns who were supposed to take care of him."

"What else have you found out?" Hatcher asked.

"He's been killing since he was a kid," Riley said. "He slit his own mother's throat when he was ten. A year later, he slit another kid's throat and burned down the orphanage. He was institutionalized for years, but he convinced everybody he was fine, including his doctor. That's why he's free now."

Hatcher nodded knowingly.

"Something's different now, isn't it?" he said. "He's changed his *modus operandi.* That's why you want to talk to me."

Riley could see that Bill was leaning forward and paying close attention now. Her partner could be disdainful, but he never had a problem appreciating whatever sources of information turned out to be valuable.

"This guy is moving faster now," Bill said. "He's not keeping his victims alive for as long."

Riley added, "And he didn't kill this latest victim the same way as the others. He did cut her throat, but not until after she was already dead."

"What was the cause of death?" Hatcher asked.

"Her neck was broken," Bill said.

Hatcher squinted his eyes with interest.

"I can tell you for sure, he didn't mean to do that. It was an accident. The throat-slitting—it's part of his ritual, he can't change it, not deliberately. So he did it afterwards, but that didn't work for him. He's losing control. He's going to move even faster now, trying to get his equilibrium back. But he can't. Nothing will work for him. Nothing will go right. He'll make mistakes."

Hatcher paused and thought for a moment.

"Don't underestimate the power of his psychosis. What he does isn't about trying to get any advantage, like money or status. It isn't about taking revenge. And he definitely doesn't do it for thrills. This guy is absolutely driven by something he doesn't understand. He may not even want to do what he's doing."

Riley realized she'd been thinking much the same thing all along.

"He's remorseful," she said.

"That's right. He feels guilty as hell. And the only way he can think of to absolve himself of all that guilt is …"

Hatcher gestured to Riley to finish his thought.

"To keep right on killing," she said. "To appease the demons driving him."

Hatcher nodded and smiled. "Smart girl. It doesn't make sense, but that's the way he is. His desperation is mounting and that might give you an advantage. He won't just disappear, go into hiding. Not for long."

Hatcher drummed his fingers and added with a slight smirk, "Whether you can catch him before he kills somebody else—well, that's up to you. Glad that's your job, not mine. That's another thing that's no part of life here in the Big House. "

Suddenly Hatcher called out, "Guard, I think we're through here."

Riley was startled. She'd expected to be able to ask a few more questions. Hatcher obviously had different ideas, and she knew better than to argue with him about it. Besides, he'd told them a lot in very short order.

Hatcher leaned across the table toward Bill and Riley.

"One more thing," he said quietly. "I can feel all the fighting going on between you two. Get over it. I'm not saying you're good for each other. You're probably bad as hell for each other. But you get good things done when you're together. That matters more in the long run than all the other stuff."

He gazed closely at Bill, then pointed to the wedding band on his finger and said, "And forget about trying to fix things with your wife. It can't be done. She'll never understand the kind of life you've chosen. Or that has chosen you."

Riley could see Bill's jaw drop with shock.

Then Hatcher turned to her and said, "And you. Stop fighting it."

Riley was on the verge of asking, *"Fighting what?"*

But no, she had to draw the line at taking personal advice from a cold-blooded murderer. That couldn't be healthy.

Not even if he's right, she thought. *And he probably is.*

"Oh, and something else," Hatcher said. "You two are just like all the cops and investigators I've ever met. You psych yourselves into thinking you're immortal, even if you know better. Don't let yourselves do that with this guy."

Hatcher's voice took on an added urgency.

"He's wounded where it hurts most—in his soul. There's nothing more dangerous than a wounded animal. Watch out. Don't get as sloppy as he's getting."

Hatcher rose from his chair and smirked again.

"He's liable to kill one of you before he's done."

Chapter 36

The next morning, Hatcher's words kept rattling through Riley's mind.

He's liable to kill one of you before he's done.

Before that, she hadn't been thinking about the chain killer as a direct threat to her or other agents. The victims he sought out, took, and murdered were of a specific type. But she knew better than to ignore Hatcher's warning. The man had uncanny insight, apparently born of years of focusing on human behavior from his special perspective in a high-security prison

Even here, in the ultra-secure Albany FBI field office, considering those words created an irrational but palpable sense of danger. It seemed almost as if Eugene Fisk was among them right here and now, unseen but poised and ready to snatch one of these agents from a desk. It didn't make sense, but there it was.

Riley was walking through the open area where agents at desks were taking phone calls, collecting tips and leads. The air was filled with phone chatter. Riley was moving from desk to desk, asking about everybody's progress—or lack of it.

At one desk, a young male agent was just ending a phone call.

"What was it about?" she asked.

The agent shook his head wearily.

"A teenaged girl over in Searcy was sure that her Uncle Joe was our guy," he said. "He fit the description. But too many details don't fit. I asked about a stutter, and he talks just fine. If what she told me is true, though, Uncle Joe is definitely a perv who ought to be behind bars. I referred her to Family Services."

"Keep at it," she said, patting him on the shoulder. "We'll get something soon."

She looked across the room at all the focused and dedicated faces, doing their best to find Eugene Fisk. As expected, hundreds of people had called the hotline number, many of them suspicious of a neighbor or relative.

Since no mention had been made to the media about a stutter, asking callers about that was a quick way to find out that the lead was false. Callers often said something like, "Well, no, he doesn't stutter, but he's a mean creep."

And of course, countless people had spotted white Ford vans up and down the Hudson River Valley. Those tips were harder to sort through, but the agents were doing their best to filter the

169

information. Lucy was also working there in the room, helping the field agents sort out plausible leads from the loads of useless chatter. They were passing any credible tips along to Bill, who had been assigned as the lead agent on the case.

Deciding that it was time to see how he was doing, Riley made her way to the temporary office Bill had been given. When she opened the door and peered inside, he gestured for her to come in.

"Anything new?" Riley asked as she walked in and sat down.

"Not a damn thing," Bill growled. "We've had five confessions so far—guys who turned themselves in in different towns. Nothing but your garden-variety attention whores."

Riley sighed with discouragement. At her best, she could get into the mind of a true serial killer. But the mind of a wannabe psychopath remained an impenetrable mystery to her. What on earth could these guys be thinking?

Just then, Lucy poked her head in the door. Her face was set with determination.

"We've got something," she said, coming into the office. "I'm afraid it's sort of a good news, bad news situation."

She gave Riley and Bill copies of a printout.

"These are transcriptions of three recorded calls," Lucy explained. "They're all from people in Talmadge, a town about halfway between here and Reedsport. Each one of these people called about a guy who calls himself Eugene Ossinger. He fits the description perfectly, right down to the stutter."

Riley skimmed the transcripts.

"I see that he drives a white Ford van," she said.

"Right," Lucy said. "It didn't occur to any of our callers to write down the license number before our bulletins got out. The van's not there now. But two of them remembered it as having Pennsylvania plates."

"Sounds like him all right," Bill said. "What's the bad news?"

Lucy sat down beside his desk.

"We also got a call directly from the Talmadge police department," she said. "One of these people had called them first. The local cops have been to the scene already, and a SWAT team too. Eugene Ossinger's not there anymore. Nobody knows where he's gone."

Riley refused to be discouraged.

"It's a start," she said. "Let's get over there right away."

About a half an hour later, Bill, Lucy, and Riley arrived in Talmadge, a little town on the west bank of the Hudson. When Bill pulled the car into the address they'd been given, the place was already taped off and surrounded by local cops and members of a SWAT team. A few neighbors were gathered nearby. Everybody seemed to be just waiting around for the FBI agents they knew were on the way.

The three agents got out of the car and strode toward the house. Bill introduced himself and his companions to the cop in charge.

"He must have known he'd been spotted," one cop told them. "He was gone before we could get here."

"Let's have a look at the premises," Riley said. They walked through the front door into a very small living room. The rest of the house included a single bedroom, a rudimentary bathroom, and a mini-kitchen. The old and worn furniture looked like it had been used by many renters.

As Riley and Lucy poked around, Bill nodded and said, "I'll go look in the basement."

Riley noticed a few signs of a recent struggle, including a broken lamp. Otherwise, everything in the house was reasonably neat and clean. The place struck Riley as a sensible choice for someone with a minuscule income. She figured that Eugene patched together a living by doing odd jobs of one kind or another. The bedroom closet held a few ragged clothes. Riley guessed that he had taken whatever he could with him, although he probably didn't have much to his name.

She heard Lucy call out from the kitchen, "There's just a little food in the refrigerator. Nothing unusual."

Riley stepped out of the bedroom just in time to see Bill come back from the basement.

"This is his place, all right," Bill said. "Come have a look."

Riley and Lucy followed Bill down a short flight of wooden steps to a bare, concrete floor.

A bloodstained cot was in the middle of the small, cell-like space. There could be no doubt about it. That was where he'd kept and tormented his victims, probably enchained and straitjacketed all during their captivity.

A strange calm settled over Riley. She was here at last, in the very heart of the killer's world. She was exactly where she needed to be.

"Give me a minute alone," she said to Bill.

Bill nodded. Of course, he understood exactly what she meant. So did Lucy by now. They both went back upstairs and shut the door behind them.

Riley took in the scene. A single overhead light was already on, probably switched on by the local police. She saw that the windows were tightly covered, so if that light was off, the room would be completely dark.

God only knew how many hours of total darkness the three women had endured in Eugene Fisk's clutches. But what the women had felt mattered little to Riley at the moment. This was her chance to learn something about what Eugene himself felt and thought, how his sick mind worked.

Riley found herself looking at a bulletin board atop a beat-up wooden table against one wall. This seemed to be a shrine of sorts. Neatly arranged on the tabletop were various items that had no doubt belonged to the women he brought here—shoes, a badge, a nametag, some buttons. Fastened to the bulletin board were all kinds of mementoes—obituaries, news stories, photos that he himself had taken of the gravesites.

Riley took a deep breath, reaching for the thoughts of the fiend who had haunted this dismal place. An insight began to take shape in inside her.

This is more than a shrine, she thought. *It's a sacred altar.*

As long as he'd held them captive, the women had been quivering, moaning, starving masses of flesh, blood, and bone. They had been under his uneasy, precarious control. But upon leaving the world, they had become avenging spirits, like the Furies of Greek legend.

Whatever items he left to appease them, whatever tears of regret he shed over this table, were all in vain. He could never, ever make amends for the suffering he had caused them.

On the opposite side of the room Riley saw another table. A rusted steel vise was fastened to the side, a vestige of long ago when it had been used as a worktable. A pegboard on the wall behind the table had once been filled with tools, but was now empty.

Riley sensed that this table, too, had a story. She went over to it and looked closely at its surface, studying strange patterns of scratches in the worn top. What were those patterns? What did they

172

spell or mean?

A vision of chains filled her mind. These were the marks left by chains. He'd kept piles of them here, sometimes coiled neatly and other times stretched out the full length of the table. He'd always handled them with the utmost reverence.

For the chains, too, were deities of a sort. Chains had ruled over him since childhood, when his mother had chained him in his own home, and again at the children's home, where the nuns had chained the door to his room shut.

He couldn't help but gather up more and more of them throughout his life. And here, right here, was where they'd called out to him, commanding him, instructing him. But like the spirits of the women, they were always unappeasable, no matter how devotedly he served them.

Riley looked back and forth between the two tables. These were both altars, and they were the twin polestars that steered his life—one an axis of guilt, shame, and repentance, and the other of impotent futility, always mocking the helpless child that he still truly was.

But unlike the table with the pictures and the mementoes, the table that had harbored the chains was now empty. What did that mean?

Riley breathed deeply, in and out, allowing herself to empathize with what Eugene was going through right now.

He'd taken the chains with him, of course. He couldn't leave them here. Without them, he'd have no purpose in life. However much he might hate what they made him do, they provided the only meaning he could cling to.

She also sensed how uprooted and lost he must feel, exiled from his sacred altars. He was alone and more desperate than ever, and the chains were doubtless furious with him. He must be frantic right now, struggling to regain some footing.

Just then she was hit by a realization. She dashed up the stairs and opened the door. Bill and Lucy were upstairs waiting for her to finish her private vigil.

"I know where we can find him," Riley said.

Chapter 37

The cemetery was silent and dark. Here, away from the drive that ran through the property, the only light came from the bright moon in the sky.

But moonlight will be enough, Riley thought. Her confidence was high.

She was looking out from behind a large marble angel with widespread wings. The sculpture stood on the hillside above a group of graves below. One of those graves was fresh. Carla Liston had been buried there that morning.

In the moonlight, Riley could easily see the walkway and the cluster of headstones below. When she and Bill had come out here a little while ago, she'd noticed a group of graves off to the right that were enclosed by a metal fence with sharp pickets. The angel she was hiding behind overlooked them all.

Riley hadn't attended the funeral that morning. She'd felt certain that Eugene wouldn't be there—not with all the media attention he'd gotten. Bill and Lucy had gone, checking out the crowd just in case, scanning for anyone resembling the computer-aged photo. Myra Cortese and several other nurses had kept watch as well. But Riley had been right, the killer wasn't there.

Instead of going to the funeral, Riley had spent her morning at the hotel with April. They were getting along well right now. Riley felt their relationship growing stronger, and she believed that this time it might last. At least, she thought, the bond felt sturdy enough to survive the rest of the teenage tumult that was certain to come.

Riley had saved her own keen watchfulness for tonight. And now here she was. Bill was also keeping watch, hidden in a grove of trees off to one side of Carla Liston's grave.

After her moment of realization in Eugene's basement, there wasn't a doubt in Riley's mind that the chain killer would show up here. She knew that those two sacred altars had given him the only meaning he had in life. The one he'd left behind made his appearance here a certainty. He simply had to find an outlet for his terrible remorse.

But the stakeout had to be conducted discreetly. Riley and Bill had decided to come here alone, taking care to remain almost invisible. Eugene would be especially vigilant right now. Even a few cops and agents stationed at the graveyard entrances would be sure to catch his attention.

Even so, the Albany office knew what Bill and Riley were up to. There were plenty of agents at strategic locations nearby, all on the lookout for Eugene or his white van. Lucy was with them, helping to coordinate their efforts. Riley was sure that she and Bill would spot Eugene—and she was equally sure that he couldn't get away.

Suddenly she heard hushed voices nearby. She whirled around and saw a young couple laughing and giggling as they approached along a path. It looked like a pair of teenagers who thought they'd found a great place to make out.

Riley stepped out from behind the marble angel and stopped them. She held out her badge in the moonlight, and put her forefinger to her lips to silence them.

The boy and the girl looked thoroughly startled. Did they realize that Riley was here looking for a killer? Riley didn't care as long as they went away. Sure enough, that's exactly what they did, turning around and quietly disappearing among the trees in the direction they'd come from.

Riley returned to her hiding place behind the angel and leaned her forehead on its wing, peering out beneath the marble feathers. The night was quiet for a long time after that.

Again, she remembered Hatcher's words …

"He's wounded where it hurts most—in his soul. There's nothing more dangerous than a wounded animal."

She also thought of something else that the Sing Sing inmate had said to her …

"Stop fighting it."

He might have meant a whole host of things—her obsession with work or her attraction to Bill, just for starters. She'd probably never know what he'd had in mind. Maybe it was just as well. And anyway, this was not the time or place to be wondering about it.

Just then she saw a movement down among the gravestones. The figure of a smallish-looking man crept stealthily along, occasionally turning on a flashlight. She drew her gun and stepped silently out from behind the angel.

The man walked up to Carla Liston's grave. He shined the flashlight on the stone, clearly checking the name. He dropped some flowers on the grave—daisies, she could see in the beam from the flashlight.

Adrenaline shot through Riley's body. The chain killer had left daisies at the grave in Reedsport. This was definitely him. Eugene

Fisk had come to show his remorse to the woman he had murdered.

His face was angled away, and Riley moved down the hillside toward him as quietly as she could. Even so, he must have heard her. He turned and looked in her direction, then whirled around and ran.

Riley took off after him. She resisted the urge to call out to Bill. She was sure that Bill had seen what was going on and was already on the move.

Riley followed the killer, weaving through the maze of headstones and statues. She was surprised by his sudden display of catlike agility. She'd long guessed that Eugene Fisk wasn't very strong, and she was probably right. But she hadn't anticipated that he was so nimble and fast. She wondered if he could even see in the dark better than she could.

She was gaining on him when she tripped over a small headstone. She staggered and almost fell flat. By the time she regained her balance, she couldn't see the killer anywhere. She stood completely still, watching and listening.

She heard movement off to one side. When she turned, she saw that it was Bill, who had been running close behind her. He, too, seemed to have lost track of the man. He stopped in his tracks.

Both Riley and Bill stood motionless, scanning the whole area. Soon there came a flicker of light that briefly revealed a figure ahead of him. The man had turned a flashlight quickly on and off to help see the path.

Riley and Bill both broke into a run toward where the light had appeared. As she ran, an image came into Riley's mind. As a little girl she'd been out catching fireflies, following the flashes in the dark. She remembered the sheer impossibility of catching an airborne firefly after seeing it flash.

Then she heard Bill cursing. He had run into the spiky metal fence that surrounded a set of graves. Riley managed to stop just before she hit the spikes herself. She cut to one side to get around the fence, and Bill headed in the other direction.

But when they got to the far side of the fenced graves, the figure they were chasing was nowhere to be seen. There was no sound or motion other than their own.

"Damn it," Riley heard Bill murmur just a few feet away from her.

He took out his cell phone and called Lucy to alert the surrounding agents that the suspect was on the move. Meanwhile,

Riley kept searching, shining her flashlight everywhere. When Bill finished talking, he also took up the search again.

Riley looked everywhere she could—behind trees, statues, some of the larger headstones, and the doorway of a mausoleum. Finally, her path converged with Bill's at a parking lot that was empty of cars. His hand was bleeding from his collision with the fence.

"Son of a bitch," he growled. "Well, he won't get far—not with so many agents all over town."

But Riley had a sinking feeling down in her gut. Their quarry's agility and swiftness had taken her completely by surprise. She also felt sure that he was too smart to have parked his van anywhere nearby. Again, she remembered how hard it was to trap a firefly in the darkness.

"No," she said to Bill, catching her breath. "We've lost him."

Chapter 38

It was dawn, and the chains were grumbling. Eugene had passed the second night huddled in the passenger seat of his van, afraid to sleep in the back where the chains might overcome him. They were angry.

"I keep telling you," he said sleepily, "there was nothing else to do."

But the muttering continued. Eugene knew that there was no point in trying to explain things all over again—that he'd been identified, and that the police would soon come to his house, and that he had to flee and take all the chains with him. Otherwise they'd be alone there. And what would happen to them when they were discovered?

Eugene twisted around, trying to get the kinks out of his weary body. After his hairbreadth escape from the graveyard last night, he ached all over. He'd had no idea that he could run so fast or so far. And he'd covered a vast obstacle course—through back yards and over fences until he could reach the van. He'd taken care not to park it near the graveyard.

He'd driven cautiously out of Albany, winding through the smallest streets and alleys, aware that cops must be on the lookout for him. He'd breathed a huge sigh of relief when he left the city on a small, southbound road and finally pulled off into a thickly wooded area to get some sleep.

Now Eugene knew he would have to go out on the road again and he had no idea where it would take him. And even though he'd disguised the van, he was still nervous about that. Years ago, realizing that a day like this might come, he'd stolen New York license plates and ordered magnetic decorations. With big colorful flowers on each side and small signs on the doors naming an imaginary business, he hoped it would pass as a florist's delivery vehicle.

He reached into the bag of food he'd brought along when he left his house. Only a single stale donut was left. He munched on it slowly.

"Where can I go?" he asked the chains.

But their murmuring was all confused, with some irritable voices saying to drive north, others to drive south, and still others telling him to head west into the Catskills. He'd never known the chains to be so quarrelsome among themselves. They'd been like this ever since he'd bungled the killing of the last woman, breaking her neck instead of slitting her throat.

He knew that it was all his fault. Everything was his fault.

Still, he had to drive somewhere. He started the van and began to pull out from among the trees. As the van rocked over the bumpy ground, the chains rattled noisily. He turned back toward them.

"What do you want now?" he demanded.

Then came a loud screeching of tires and the blare of a car horn. He braked hard and brought the van to a stop. Because of the chains' distracting rattle, he'd pulled out onto the road in front of an approaching car.

Now the driver was staring at him in shocked and angry surprise. Eugene swerved his van into the far lane and continued on his way.

Forcing himself to pay attention, he drove slowly past a few houses, a restaurant, and a post office. He hoped that nobody in the little village would notice him. When the road was again lined by trees, he relaxed a little.

But the chains were agitated again. They wanted something. They always wanted something.

In a few moments, he saw a woman walking toward him along the side of the road. She was wearing white. He thought it looked like a waitress uniform. She wasn't a nurse or a guard like the others, but still ...

"Her?" he asked the chains.

He heard them murmur with approval.

He pulled onto the shoulder and stopped his van, but left the motor running. He got out, went around to the back and opened the doors. He picked up a heavy handful of chains.

By that time, the woman was walking past him on the edge of the road.

"Do you have some sort of problem?" she asked, stepping toward him with a polite smile. "There's a repair shop ..."

But then her expression froze with horror. She recognized him. Just as she turned to run, Eugene smashed the chains into the side of her head. She fell to her knees with a cry, and he hit her again. He caught the unconscious woman beneath her arms. Fortunately she was small enough and light enough for him to handle. He dragged her into the van and scrambled back into the driver's seat.

"I hope you'll be happier now," he said to the chains.

But as he drove, a new wave of despair began to sweep over

him. How could he possibly deal with this woman in a manner that would fully quell the chains? For one thing, he had no place to keep her. He'd have to kill her much too quickly. And where could he even do it? Where could he take her now?

The road still wound among trees. After a time it bent to the right, led across railroad tracks, and ended at an old marina. There was a ramshackle pier with a couple of old fishing boats tied to it. A massive rusted steel structure loomed over the pier.

When he realized what the structure was, Eugene laughed aloud. He could hardly believe his luck. It was an old boat crane, used to lift small yachts and place them in the water. It didn't look like it had been used for a long time, but there was still a pulley up there on its arm. A cable ran through the pulley and dangled to the ground. It would be easy to hang the woman up here, where she could be found by her family and neighbors.

It would require outrageous daring, to do all this in the daylight.

So much the better, he thought.

Maybe the chains would be impressed.

To be sure that no watchers were nearby, he walked out onto the pier. He had to move carefully because some of the boards were missing and others were obviously weak. When he reached the end, he turned and surveyed the shore.

No one was in sight. He looked out over the water. A few boats were out there on the Hudson, but most were too far away to notice him. Someone on the craft nearest him did wave in a friendly manner. Eugene waved back and watched the boat move away. Letters on the side spelled *Suzy.*

The Suzy, he thought. *What would it be like to be out there on a boat called the* Suzy?

Standing on the pier's end, Eugene was seized by a strange craving. If he had a boat and could go out on the water, could the chains follow him? How could they?

Out there he might be free. He couldn't remember what it felt like to be free.

Two old boats were tied up at the pier. They were both floating and seaworthy. Could he get one of the engines going and sail away from here forever?

But then he heard a loud groan from the van. The woman was starting to regain consciousness. He had to go subdue her and put her into a straitjacket and chains. Then he had to go through with

180

the rest of his horrible task. The chains gave him no choice. They never would give him a choice.

Chapter 39

Riley knew in her gut that something was about to break. She didn't know why she felt that way. They'd chosen their route on the basis of some pretty scanty information. Bill was driving, and the three of them were headed south from Albany.

After Eugene Fisk's escape from the graveyard yesterday, the public was responding to bulletins with more calls than ever. Field agents had spread out in all directions trying to follow up on anything that seemed at least remotely plausible. There had been a cluster of sightings reported on the highways south of Albany, and Bill, Riley, and Lucy had decided to head out in that direction.

"How far we from Callaway?" Lucy asked from the back seat.

Riley turned and saw that Lucy was looking at a text message. It was probably an update from the Albany office.

"We just passed a turnoff for Callaway," Bill said.

"We need to go back and take it," Lucy said.

Without asking any questions, Bill slowed the vehicle and turned it around. As he drove, Lucy explained the tip she had received.

"A man in Callaway said some crazy guy pulled out from nowhere on the road in front of his car. It was a white delivery van for a business called June's Flowers. The man got a good look at the driver. He swears it's our man, and that he was headed toward an old marina. Everybody in the town has been notified to stay away from there."

Riley's heart quickened. Yes, this was it. She was sure of it. The business name came as no surprise at all. Everyone at Albany's HQ knew perfectly well that Eugene Fisk had probably disguised his van by now.

"Lucy, send a return message that we're on our way," Bill said, making the turn that he'd passed by a few moments before. "We're liable to need backup. Riley, check the GPS to see what we're driving into."

Riley brought up the map on her cell phone. She was heartened by what she saw.

"We're on the right road," she said. "It goes through Callaway, then straight to the marina. It ends in a cull-de-sac. If Eugene Fisk went there, this road is his only way out."

Bill put his foot on the accelerator as the siren blared.

He slowed down when they crossed the town line into

Callaway. A few anxious-looking residents stood on the sidewalk watching them go by. On the far side of the village, local police had set up a roadblock. Bill held up his FBI badge and they waved him on through. He sped up again and in a matter of minutes, the marina came in sight.

Bill brought the car to a stop and turned off the siren.

Riley's heart pumped faster. There it was, parked beside a rusted crane-like structure—a white van decorated with flowers and the business name June's Flowers. The three agents jumped out of the car and headed for the van. Bill got there first and yanked the rear door open.

A woman was huddled on the floor, bound with a straitjacket and chains. Her eyes opened and she moaned aloud through the chain that had been wrapped around her face to gag her.

She's alive, Riley thought with relief. They had gotten here in time.

But there was no sign of Eugene Fisk.

"Lucy, take care of the woman," Riley said. "Bill and I will find him."

Riley headed around the van to search the shoreline, but she stopped at the sound of Bill's voice.

"Riley!"

She turned and looked at him. His eyes met Riley's with a determined and yet sympathetic expression.

"This guy is not Peterson," Bill said.

For a second, Riley couldn't understand what he meant.

"What?" she said.

Bill narrowed his eyes and said much more slowly, "He's not Peterson."

In a moment of clarity, Riley understood exactly what he meant. Her use of deadly force against Peterson had bordered on vengefulness. But the Bureau hadn't raised questions about it—not after all she'd suffered at Peterson's hands. This situation was different. They should be able to bring in Eugene Fisk alive.

This kind of instantaneous communication was one thing she treasured most about working with Bill. She'd missed it during their estrangement.

"I understand," she told him.

Guns in hand, Riley and Bill moved around the van. There was a drop to the water. Along the high ground, clusters of trees could easily hide the killer. Riley was sure they were close to him now.

She moved carefully toward the trees on the left. Bill moved off to the right.

Riley had realized that the killer wasn't where she was searching when she heard Lucy's voice call out, "I see him!"

Riley turned and saw that Lucy was headed away from the van. She had drawn her weapon and was running toward the pier. The horrible little man was a few yards out on the old structure.

"Stop right there!" Lucy called out to him, her weapon raised. "Hands where I can see them!"

Eugene stopped and turned, his hands raised above his head. In one hand he was clutching a bundle of chains.

Riley drew her own weapon and walked toward them. She felt a flood of relief. This was going to end easily and without violence. What had happened with Peterson was not going to happen here.

Lucy stepped out onto the pier, focused intently on Eugene. But after a few steps, a rotting board broke out from under her, and she fell into a tangle.

"Damn it!" Lucy cried out.

Eugene moved with the same dexterity and speed that he'd shown at the graveyard. In an instant, he grabbed and held Lucy from behind. He wrapped the chain around her neck with one hand. With the other had he took a straight-edged razor out of his pocket. He flipped open the blade and held it at Lucy's throat. Her face was contorted with pain.

Eugene was trying desperately to talk.

"Drop—drop—"

Riley knew that he was trying to tell her to drop her weapon. She wasn't ready to do that.

Lucy let out a scream of pain as Eugene pulled her loose from the broken board. He forced her forward along the pier back toward the shore. It looked like her ankle was broken.

"Let—let me—"

Riley understood. The chain killer wanted to take Lucy back to his van as a hostage and drive out of here undisturbed.

She heard Bill's voice from nearby.

"Easy, easy," he was saying to Eugene. "You can't get out of here. You know that."

But Riley saw that neither she nor Bill had a feasible shot. Lucy's body formed too effective a shield.

"Let—let me—" Eugene said again. He was on the shore now and backing toward the van with his hostage.

Bill was standing beside Riley, his Glock raised.

Riley's thoughts clicked away as she tried to assess the situation. She knew one thing for certain. Eugene Fisk wasn't bluffing with the razor. He'd slit women's throats before, and he'd do it again in an instant if either Riley or Bill made the wrong move.

Shane Hatcher had been exactly right.

He's liable to kill one of you before he's done.

Riley glanced over at Bill.

"Stand down, Bill," she said.

Bill looked at her with surprise. But then he lowered his weapon.

Riley stooped and placed her weapon on the ground.

"I'm putting down my gun, Eugene," she said. "You can let her go. We can end this peacefully."

But Eugene was shaking his head.

"N—no," he stammered. He was still determined to make his escape with Lucy as a hostage. He continued dragging Lucy toward the van.

Riley looked directly into his eyes. He stared back, unable to break their gaze, as if hypnotized. His eyes were small and beady, but Riley saw terrible worlds in them—worlds of childhood suffering and adult humiliation, of pain both physical and emotional, and of almost unfathomable self-loathing.

"He's not Peterson," Bill had said just a few minutes ago.

Riley now knew that Bill had been more right than he'd realized.

Eugene Fisk was the most pitiable monster she'd ever encountered. And she could turn that insight to her advantage.

As Eugene waddled backwards dragging Lucy along, Riley moved slowly in the same direction.

"I know about the chains, Eugene," Riley said in a sympathetic voice. "I hear them too. You're not alone. You're not the only person who hears them. I do too."

Eugene stopped in his tracks. He looked positively stricken now. Riley was getting to him. She knew it.

She remembered something else that Shane Hatcher had said.

"He's wounded where it hurts most—in his soul."

And I'm probing that wound, Riley realized.

"Don't you hear what they're saying now, Eugene—the chains?" Riley went on. "They're saying it's over. You've uprooted them, you've failed them for the last time, and they're through with you. It's really over. The chains are saying so. I hear them. You do too."

Those small eyes were getting larger now. They glistened with tears.

"The chains don't want you to take this woman," Riley said. "She isn't what they need."

Eugene nodded with understanding.

"You know what the chains want you to do instead," Riley said.

Eugene nodded again.

Then he drew the blade across his own throat and sliced it deeply, all the way across.

Riley heard herself scream.

Eugene fell to the ground, clutching his throat, gurgling and coughing. Lucy was drenched in his spurting blood, but she was free of him now. She fell too, but rolled away from the wounded killer.

Riley threw herself upon Eugene as he twitched and writhed. Her hands fumbled around his throat, trying to staunch the bleeding, to plug up the rapidly escaping breath. It was no good. There was nothing she could do. His eyes were wide open, fearful and fading. In a matter of seconds, he lay motionless. She knew that he was dead.

Bill was standing at her side. He reached down and tried to help her to her feet.

"Come on," he said. "We've got to take care of the woman."

But Riley found that she couldn't stand.

"I killed him," she said.

"You did what you had to do," Bill said.

"No," Riley said. "I killed him."

She broke down and sobbed as the sound of approaching sirens filled the air.

186

Chapter 40

As she looked around her new townhouse, Riley felt freer, luckier, and richer than she ever had, even in the elegant house she used to share with Ryan. This home, after all, was hers.

Even so, something was troubling her deep down.

What is it? she wondered.

She couldn't put her finger on it.

Without a doubt, this place was better than Riley had dreamed of. The main floor of the house was open, with the living and dining area flowing together and a large deck at the back. The kitchen was fabulous, more than Riley thought she would ever need, but Gabriela loved it.

And it had been Gabriela's room that had really sold the house to Riley. The basement room that opened to the little back yard had been converted into what the real estate agent called an "in-law suite." It was a big carpeted room with a gas fireplace and a private bathroom.

Gabriela was down there now, unpacking and organizing her things.

April came wandering out of the kitchen, munching on a sandwich.

"How are you coming with getting your room organized?" Riley asked.

"It's so big!" she said, beaming. "It's like twice the size of what I had! And so is the closet!"

Riley smiled, feeling happy for the first time in a long time. Feeling like a real mom.

"So is it ready for me to see yet?" Riley asked.

"Not yet. Just a few more things to put away. Then I'll need your help hanging some things on the wall."

"Just let me know when."

April swallowed the last of her sandwich. Then she said, "Mom."

"Yes."

"Mom, I love it! I love this house. I love my room."

"And I love you," Riley said, giving her daughter a hug.

April hugged her back and then scampered away upstairs.

Riley drew a deep breath of relief. Not only did her daughter love the new house, but she was once again the bubbly teenager who had been missing for months now.

She had been lucky to find the house on a tip from a co-worker before it actually went on the market. The drive to Quantico would only take her thirty minutes, and April would be able to get around by public transportation—no more hitchhiking ever. And she wouldn't have to change schools.

It certainly marked a new beginning, the start of a different life. She felt confident that it would be a better life for both April and herself. Her divorce was final, and Ryan was paying the support that he had promised. Riley and April both understood that their contact with Ryan would most likely be civil but infrequent. Riley thought that would probably be best for all of them.

Ryan had already moved on to a more suitable liaison, a divorced D.C. society woman who could support him in every way. Riley wouldn't be surprised if he moved closer to Washington sometime soon.

Yes, Riley thought, *this will suit all of us fine—April, Gabriela, and me.*

Still, some nagging discord kept whispering through her brain. She decided to ignore it. She looked around, thinking about where she would need to fill in with a new piece of furniture here and there.

Her thoughts were interrupted by the front doorbell. When she answered the door, Bill was standing outside.

"Just thought I'd stop by and see your new place," he said.

Riley could tell by his forced smile and his ragged, tired look that he was here for more than that.

"What's wrong?" she asked.

"Can I come in?" Bill said.

"Of course."

Bill came inside and the two of them sat down on the couch.

"Maggie is filing for divorce," Bill said. "I've already moved out, into an apartment near the BAU."

"I'm sorry," Riley said.

Bill shook his head with confusion and dismay.

"It's just that I've tried so damn hard for so many years," he said. "It's weird to think that it's really all over. Maggie and I have been strangers for a long time. But the kids … I don't want to be a stranger to my boys."

Riley patted his hand.

"You won't be," she said.

"You don't know that," he said.

188

Riley sighed. Bill was right. She didn't know anything of the kind. There were far too many things in life that she didn't know.

Bill seemed eager to change the subject.

"That last case," he began, then shook his head and sighed. She could see that it was still haunting him, too. In some ways it was comforting to see she was not the only one who was haunted. "Have we ever dealt with one that twisted?"

Riley thought for a moment.

"Twisted? No, that's not exactly right. He was the most damaged, though."

"Damaged, twisted, take your pick," Bill said, shaking his head. "Chains and straitjackets and a straight razor—it's a new combination for me."

Riley remembered her experience of the chain killer's mind.

"Eugene was the most reluctant killer I've known," she said. "But he would never have stopped if we hadn't caught up with him."

"And we did stop him," Bill said. "We're good at that. Together, we're very good."

*

After a short while, Bill left. He'd said he didn't want to bother Riley when things were going so well for her. She'd protested that he was no bother, that he was never a bother and never would be, but he went away anyhow.

As she watched him drive off, she thought about what a deeply decent man he was. She was lucky to have him as a partner and a friend. Whatever happened between them in the days ahead, she hoped their friendship wouldn't be ruined. They'd come too close to losing it already.

Then she walked through her house and out onto the back deck. Several houses down, children were playing in the yard. Riley had longed for exactly this—a bustling neighborhood where people went about normal lives in an ordinary way.

What was missing? What was wrong?

Then she remembered—she still had trouble looking into a mirror. The faces of all those victims and monsters kept looking back. And now there was Eugene's face also, his beady eyes full of hurt, guilt, and self-hatred. She'd understood what had gone on behind those eyes only too well. And as horrible a man as he was, his fate still haunted her.

She had merely fought with Peterson and killed him in a primal way, in a blur of self preservation, for herself and for her daughter.

With Eugene, she had used her powers of empathy and understanding.

With Eugene, she had used deadly force.

And not a person in the world could understand that except Riley.

She knew that more monsters lurked out there in the world, probably in more variations that even she had yet imagined. It was her job to stop them. But what would she do the next time she faced those who tormented and destroyed?

She remembered what Hatcher had told her.

"Stop fighting it."

She still didn't know what "it" was—but she was starting to think that it was something huge, maybe as big as her whole life. And what did it mean that a multiple murderer understood something about her that she didn't know herself?

Her cell phone interrupted her questions. She saw that the call was from Brent Meredith. She knew he wasn't calling just to find out how the move was going.

Her heart beat faster. He was calling about a new case.

She stood there and looked at her buzzing cell phone. She turned and looked away, looked out the window, down the block, at her new house—anywhere but at the phone.

Yet still, it kept consistently buzzing. It was like her life, like the flood of cases that never ended, always buzzing at her.

Stop fighting it.

Had he meant fighting the urge to take on a case? Or had he meant something else? Fighting having a life? Living life for the first time?

Riley watched her phone buzz, again and again.

This time, she was not so quick to answer it.

And she did not know if she would again.

COMING IN MAY, 2016!

ONCE CRAVED
(A Riley Paige Mystery—Book #3)

ONCE CRAVED is book #3 in the bestselling Riley Paige mystery series, which begins with ONCE GONE (Book #1)--a free download with over 100 five star reviews!

When prostitutes turn up dead in Phoenix, not much attention is paid. But when a pattern of disturbing murders is discovered, the local police soon realize a serial killer is on a rampage and they are in way over their heads. Given the unique nature of the crimes, the FBI, called in, knows they will need their most brilliant mind to crack the case: Special Agent Riley Paige.

Riley, recovering from her last case and trying to pick up the pieces of her life, is at first reluctant. But when she learns of the grievous nature of the crimes and realizes the killer will soon strike again, she is compelled. She begins her hunt for the elusive killer and her obsessive nature takes her too far—perhaps too far, this time, to pull herself back from the brink.

Riley's search leads her into the unsettling world of prostitutes, of broken homes, and shattered dreams. She learns that, even amongst these women, there are glimpses of hope, hope being robbed by a violent psychopath. When a teenage girl is abducted, Riley, in a frantic race against time, struggles to probe the depths of the killer's mind. But what she discovers leads her to a twist that is too shocking for even her to imagine.

A dark psychological thriller with heart-pounding suspense, ONCE CRAVED is book #3 in a riveting new series—with a beloved new character—that will leave you turning pages late into the night.

Book #4 in the Riley Paige series will be available soon.

BOOKS BY BLAKE PIERCE

RILEY PAIGE MYSTERY SERIES

ONCE GONE (Book #1)
ONCE TAKEN (Book #2)
ONCE CRAVED (Book #3)

Blake Pierce

Blake Pierce is author of the bestselling RILEY PAGE mystery series, which include the mystery suspense thrillers ONCE GONE (book #1), ONCE TAKEN (book #2) and ONCE CRAVED (#3).

An avid reader and lifelong fan of the mystery and thriller genres, Blake loves to hear from you, so please feel free to visit www.blakepierceauthor.com to learn more and stay in touch.

Manufactured by Amazon.ca
Bolton, ON

17025997R00116